SHE'S LEAVING HOME

Colette is fed up with her mother nagging about school and her future. And she's fed up with her mother's boyfriend too. And as for her fashion sense, if it wasn't so embarrassing, Colette would find it funny.

But Colette's mum is not the only parent causing embarrassment at St Andrews Road School parents' evening. Sam's mother is treating the whole thing like a military operation. She's even brought her clipboard. And Dim's mother has been told not to speak unless spoken to. For Colette, parents' night is bad enough, but there's worse to come. And being accused of pinching £60 by her own mother is the final straw. Moving into a squat – Jules's suggestion – sounds like a good idea. And in some ways it is – though not for any reasons Colette can guess.

This is the third book in the S.T.A.R.S. sequence. Every month there will be a new, self-contained story, all about the same group of sixth formers. S.T.A.R.S. is based on reality, taking you inside a modern London comprehensive. Join now. The common-room door is always open. Waiting for you . . .

Hunter Davies is an author, journalist and broadcaster. He has written over thirty books, ranging from biographies of the Beatles to William Wordsworth, and he wrote the 'Father's Day' column in *Punch* for ten years. He is the author of the *Flossie Teacake* stories and has also written a book for teenagers, *Saturday Night*. He has three children and lives in London.

STARS
ST ANDREWS ROAD SCHOOL

She's Leaving Home

HUNTER DAVIES

PENGUIN BOOKS

PENGUIN BOOKS

Published by the Penguin Group
27 Wrights Lane, London W8 5TZ, England
Viking Penguin Inc., 40 West 23rd Street, New York, New York 10010, USA
Penguin Books Australia Ltd, Ringwood, Victoria, Australia
Penguin Books Canada Ltd, 2801 John Street, Markham, Ontario,
Canada L3R 1B4
Penguin Books (NZ) Ltd, 182–190 Wairau Road, Auckland 10, New Zealand

Penguin Books Ltd, Registered Offices: Harmondsworth, Middlesex, England

First published 1989
1 3 5 7 9 10 8 6 4 2

Filmset in Linotron Ehrhardt by
Rowland Phototypesetting Ltd,
Bury St Edmunds, Suffolk
Printed and bound in Great Britain by
Cox and Wyman Ltd, Reading, Berks.

Sam: lagging behind

EPISODE 1

St Andrews Road, early evening

Colette and her mother are heading towards St Andrews Road School. Colette is walking as quickly as possible, just in case she might be seen with her mother.

'I told you not to wear those high heels,' says Colette. 'You look really stupid.'

'Slow down, darling,' says her mother. 'It's not a race.'

'Oh yes it is,' says Colette. 'It's a race to get this over as quickly as possible. I hate these evenings. And I hate you coming with me. There's no need for it at all. I've told you before.'

'But I want to,' says her mother. 'I'm concerned about your future.'

'I've decided not to have a future,' says Colette. 'It's been cancelled. The future is off the menu. Sold out. So you can go straight home and see that

5

toy boy of yours, which is what I know you want to do anyway. Don't kid on you're interested, you never have been, not in me . . .'

Colette's mother smiles. She has heard all this before, umpteen times. It is an act, partly to provoke and partly to hide Colette's nervousness. She suspects that the evening ahead might have a few shocks in store for her daughter.

'Oh Gawd,' exclaims Colette, turning round. 'I've just seen your jeans. Did I or did I not warn you about them? Wear your baggy ones, if you must, not those skin-tight stretch ones. You look disgusting. Ugh, really gross. At your age, you should *never* wear that sort of stuff.'

'I do apologize, dear,' says her mother. 'I only wish I had your fashion sense. Perhaps you'll tell me some of your secrets one day . . .'

'Huh,' grunts Colette. They walk in silence for a while.

'I do think you should have worn some sort of jacket,' says her mother.

'I haven't got a bloody jacket!'

'No need to swear,' says her mother. 'All it shows is a lack of vocabulary.'

'But you know I haven't got a jacket. I've got no money, so how can I buy a jacket?'

'You have that lovely long woollen one, I've always liked that, and the tweed jacket you got from Camden Lock which you never wear.'

'All horrible.'

'Well you could have borrowed something of mine.'

'And looked like a proper jerk.'

'It'll be cold when we come out, you know. Can you feel a nip in the air? It really is the season of mists and mellow fruitfulness.'

'Spare me all that poetic rubbish,' says Colette. 'I had enough of that junk when we were doing GCSE.'

'When I was in the sixth form –' begins her mother.

'Not again,' groans Colette. She walks quickly ahead but her mother catches her up, almost falling, thanks to her heels.

'When I was in the sixth form, we never had these sort of evenings. You're so lucky. In my day, teachers never met parents. They were superior beings, unaccountable, unapproachable. Everything was left to them. I don't even remember applying to university. It just sort of happened . . .'

'Like me, you mean,' says Colette.

'Now that is unkind,' says her mother. 'And untrue. You know that.'

'Sorry,' says Colette, stopping and taking her mother's arm. They walk in silence again, but a more friendly silence.

'You're not nervous about this evening, are you?' asks her mother.

'Course not,' says Colette. 'Only about you.'

They stop at the school gates. Colette turns to face her mother. 'Right, if you are insisting on coming in, then there's one condition.'

'What's that, dear?'

'Keep your gob shut. Is that clear? I'll do all the

talking. Right? Tonight, you have the non-speaking part. Okay?'

Her mother nods her head.

'Right, we'll go in then.'

Further down St Andrews Road

Sam and his parents have just left their large Victorian home in a tree-lined street off St Andrews Road. Sam is lagging behind, dragging his feet, huffing and puffing, moaning and groaning. His mother is bounding ahead, eager for the evening and carrying a clipboard.

'Right, you'll take European History and Human Geography,' says Sam's mother to her husband, who is trying to keep up with her. 'I'll take English History and Sociology. I want to meet this famous Mr Grott. There's something I want to ask, and I can't leave that to you.'

She stops, checks her clipboard, takes her pen out of its holder which hangs on a leather thong round her neck.

'Sorry, what was that?' says her husband.

'Please do concentrate,' says Sam's mother. 'Look, on my list. I've ticked the times and the names and which of us is doing which. There will be a plan of the hall, so we'll know where everyone is sitting the moment we get in. You can then go straight off and do your teachers. Is that clear?'

'Look, I don't really need to come,' says Sam, catching up with them. 'I'm not really necessary.'

'They probably won't be running to time,' says his mother to her husband, ignoring Sam. 'They never do, so if queues build up at one place, be prepared to move around.'

'It's like a military operation,' says Sam's father.

'If you had come all the other times,' says his mother, 'you would know about it. This is the only way to tackle it; divide and conquer, otherwise we'll be there for ages and the staff get more and more tired as the evening wears on.'

'There's a programme on the telly I wanna watch,' says Sam. 'If I miss it, it'll be your fault.'

'What about the headmaster? What's he called, Mr Wainwright,' says Sam's father. 'Will you see him or should I?'

'Typical,' says his mother. 'He retired three years ago. Just shows you how much you've missed.'

'Gracious, never knew that. Who's the new bloke?'

'Woman,' corrects Sam's mother. 'Mrs Potter.'

'Not Pansy Potter, the Strong Man's Daughter.'

'And don't make that sort of joke this evening,' says Sam's mother. 'It just dates you.'

'Wrong there, darling,' says her husband. '*Dandy* and *Beano* are now collector's items. Old ones cost a fortune. Wish I could get more of them for my stall. They're brilliant comics. Sam still reads them, don't you, Sam?'

'Never stop,' says Sam. 'In fact I really should be studying them this evening. Mr Grott's given us a project on popular culture and popular prejudice, so if you don't mind I'll go home now and –'

'You certainly will not,' says his mother. 'I want none of your nonsense.'

'Sorry Mum.'

'Oh no!' says his mother. 'I've just seen his feet. Look at them! You really are a disgrace. I thought I threw those trainers in the dustbin. Do you mean to say you grovelled in there and got them out?'

Sam grunts. They walk in silence till they come to the school gates. As they enter, bang on time, Sam's mum looks at her watch, checks the clipboard for the last time, then looks again at her son's horrible trainers.

'I should have sent you home to change,' she says. 'Just try to keep your feet hidden, that's all. And don't pick at the soles, as you usually do.'

'Anything else?' says Sam, wearily.

'Yes, don't mumble when teachers speak to you.'

'Hmmmmmm,' Sam mumbles.

'And don't forget,' says his mother. 'We are doing this for your sake.'

The school gates, a few minutes later

A very battered Ford Cortina draws up, coughing and spluttering. The driver, unshaven and pot-bellied, gets out, also coughing and spluttering. He opens the near-side back door, carefully. It is broken and can only be opened from the outside as the hinge has gone. The door needs to be watched in case it finally falls off.

Dim gets out of the back seat, then goes round to the other door and helps out his mother. She is dressed all in black, her best going-out clothes, though she hardly goes out anywhere. Despite two decades in London, it is still a foreign city to her.

The driver, who is Dim's dad, stands and hesitates, forgetting for a moment that he is not waiting to be paid. He mutters in Greek to his wife, asking if she'll be all right, then gets back in the car, about to begin another evening's work.

'This your school, then?' says Dim's mother, as they walk through the school gates together. Dim nods.

'Is very big, innit,' she says.

'Yeah, there's about a thousand pupils.'

'A thousand?' says his mother, surprised.

This is her very first visit to Dim's school. A week ago, Dim happened to take home the school's weekly Bulletin, listing all the coming events. It has come out every week for most of the three years which Mrs Potter has been at St Andrews Road School, but Dim usually chucks it away. This time he had written some vital information on the back which he wanted to keep – the latest bank and building-society interest rates.

His mother found the Bulletin in Dim's jeans' pocket, just as she was about to wash them, and wanted to know what it was all about. Not the bank rates, she has managed to survive without them, but all these things happening at Dim's school. When she heard parents were invited tonight, she decided to come, knowing her husband never would.

'Is too big,' says his mother as they walk down the drive to the front door of the New Building. It is a door which during the day is traditionally reserved for staff and sixth formers. This is one of the very few sixth-form privileges left over from the grammar-school years, apart from having their own common room.

'It's not really too big. Our sixth form is sort of separate, and we only have 200 people,' says Dim. 'Look, I'll explain it all another time. Just follow me around. Don't ask no questions. All right?'

'What you say, Dim,' says his mother, smiling.

Still at the school gates

A black cab arrives, a proper London taxi. Out of it jumps Jules.

'You don't want me to sign, do you?' he asks the driver. 'It is on the account.'

'That's all right, guv,' says the man, doing a U-turn in the road and driving off.

'Oh my Gawd, look who it is!' Almost in unison, four voices shout out the same words.

Kirsty and Ella, arm in arm, are arriving at the gates, just as Raffy and Toby appear from the opposite direction. All of them are exclaiming at the sight of Jules, as he suddenly bounces on to the pavement in front of them.

'What a flash bastard you are, Jules,' says Raffy.

'Jealousy could get you somewhere,' says Jules. 'Actually, it's my dad's business account. I have to use it up or he might get it taken away. He's always in his company car, so he makes me order as many cabs as I can, just to help. Such a bore.'

'Oh shurrup, Jules,' says Kirsty. 'We don't wanna hear any more.'

'And try to keep your clothes quiet,' says Colette.

'Glad you mentioned them, darling,' says Jules. 'I

always feel that parents' evenings are just so drab, don't you, hmm? One must do one's best to brighten them up. If we can't have inward sparkle, let's have some exterior brightness.'

Jules has excelled himself. For most of the term so far he has been in high-society summer wear, or his version of it, going in for faded twenties blazers, baggy flannels, straw boaters and patent-leather shoes. This evening, he has remained sportive, but has adopted what he would describe as a more modern metaphor. He is wearing a white tracksuit bottom, white designer trainers, a violently coloured baseball sweatshirt and a peaked baseball cap. Flash it certainly is. He gives a few twirls, so they can get the benefit of every carefully chosen item.

Kirsty and Colette give a few affected yells and screams, then they link his arms as they walk through the school gates and down the drive. Another scream suddenly comes from Raffy, of pure jealousy this time, with no attempt to hide it.

'Oh my God!' shouts Raffy. 'Look at his hat!'

Out of Jules's baseball cap shoots a little radio aerial. Hanging down from either side above each ear is an earphone, like those on a Walkman.

'It's like something from Startrek,' says Kirsty.

'What a poser,' says Toby.

'Is it real?' asks Ella.

'Oh *this*,' says Jules, all nonchalant. He reaches up to the front of the cap, touches what appears to be a school badge and presses a button. He listens, then starts swaying to the music.

'Jazz saxophone. Courtney Pine, I think,' he says,

taking his cap off. 'Would you like to hear it, Ella? You might get some tips.'

'I'm not doing the saxophone any more,' says Ella. But she accepts his offer of a listen, putting on the cap and adjusting the earphones. 'Hey,' she says. 'It's excellent.'

In turn, they all have a go, remarking on the good reception, the neat arrangement, the clever idea. Only Toby refuses to try the hat out, dismissing it as a silly gimmick.

'You're such a lucky git,' says Raffy. 'Can I borrow it for tomorrow? I could wear it when I go to see Banks. Tell you what, I'll buy it from you if I ever get any money.'

'Where did you get it from, Jules?' says Kirsty. 'I've never seen one before.'

'My old man,' says Jules. 'He went to this trade show. They were just giving them away. There were huge sacks of them, and you could just help yourself.'

'Oh no, don't go on,' says Raffy. 'If only my gran would go to trade shows. If only my gran went anywhere. She's got no contacts at all. That's why she wears specs.'

They all laugh at Raffy. It is only recently that he has let it be known that he lives with his grandmother, the woman who brought him up. In the lower years at school, he carefully kept it quiet.

Jules has been sending himself up, overdoing the flashness, but Toby, who only arrived in the sixth form this term and has still not got the measure of Jules, has not quite understood the joke.

'I think it's ridiculous,' says Toby. 'Conspicuous consumption.'

'Isn't that what they died of in Victorian times?' asks Kirsty.

'Hey, you've got a point there,' says Raffy. 'Jules doesn't look at all healthy to me. Recent research has shown that too much listening to a radio hat makes you sterile.'

'Is that true, Raffy?' says Ella, half believing him.

'Straight up,' says Raffy. 'Here, let me take it off you, Jules.' He tries to grab the hat from Jules, but Jules pushes him away. They then all push and shove each other, playing silly buggers as they go through the main door, tripping and falling over each other.

'Lively tonight are we, Raphael?'

It is Mr Banks, Deputy Headmaster, standing inside the front foyer with his best suit on and his most polished smile, ready to greet parents.

'Oh, there's a good chap,' says Raffy, pretending to put a coin in Mr Banks's hand. 'Go and park the Roller for me. It's the white one, you can't miss it.'

Mr Banks gives a strained grin, then manages a much better smile as he sees Kirsty, one of the few sixth-form girls he ever seems to have time for.

'No parents, hmm?' enquires Mr Banks.

'No, mater can't make it,' says Raffy. 'She's in the operating theatre – usual dramas. Who'd be a consultant at the Royal Free . . .'

There are no smiles. Mr Banks knows the truth about Raffy's parents from the school records, as they all do.

'Sorry,' says Toby. 'My parents just can't make it tonight. They send their apologies.' Much to Toby's relief. He doesn't want them to see the inside of his new school, which he chose himself. They might be horrified at the comparison with his old one, Westminster. Even more important, he doesn't want his new friends to see his parents. Not yet, anyway.

'My dad's working,' explains Ella. This is not the whole truth. She forced him to do a night shift tonight, against his will. He was desperate to come to school in the hope of picking up any information on his daughter's activities, but that is the last thing Ella wants.

'Mine are busy,' says Kirsty, simpering. Busy watching television. Kirsty's parents did come to her school once, in the first year, but felt out of it and have never come again. Much to Kirsty's relief.

And so in to school they go, four students, parentless, about to join the hordes already with their parents, to hear the very latest from the front line.

Raffy: 'Where's Taz?'

EPISODE 2

The school hall,
sixth-form parents' meeting

The main hall has been divided up into about thirty different areas, each with a table. There is a member of staff in each area, sitting at the table, with three chairs vacant, one for a student and the other two for the student's parents or guardians, should they turn up. There is a hand-written notice on each table, with a number, the name of the teacher and the subject. At least there was at the beginning of the evening. Now that the meeting has begun, many of the notices have already fallen off and been lost in the crush.

Some of the foyers, corridors and smaller rooms leading off the hall are also being used, which leads

17

to lots of confusion. Non-regular visitors to such open evenings at the school don't know where to find some subjects and stand around lost, consulting their duplicated plan of the hall given out on arrival.

At the far end of the hall, light refreshments are being served, handed through from the kitchen. On the stage at the other end of the room sit Mrs Potter, the Head, and Lionel Witting, Head of Sixth, ready to discuss matters of a more general, non-curricular nature.

Viewed from above, should you be hanging from the ceiling, the scene in the hall resembles an ant hill, with streams of little creatures pouring in one direction, then stopping, going off in another, forming new queues, only to break up and start all over again.

In one of the few cool calm corners, cut off from the maelstrom, stand Raffy and Jules, looking cool and calm. They are at the refreshments end, enjoying a glass of white wine. It is cheap and nasty stuff, poured from what looks like petrol cans by members of the PTA. The wine is for parents, to give a certain social flavour to the evening, draw the parents in, and prove that state schools do have a human face these days. But almost to a man, and a woman, they are busy elsewhere, jostling at the tables, eager to be seen, eager to be heard, eager for any news about the present progress of their offspring. Most of all, they are eager, if not desperate, to hear any good news about the possible future progress of their beloveds.

'Pretty sickening, isn't it?' says Raffy, staring at the crowds. Jules does not reply, his attention elsewhere.

'Okay then, if you insist, Jules,' continues Raffy, 'I will have another glass of paint stripper.'

'Actually, I think it's fascinating,' says Jules, buying two more drinks. 'I love these evenings. Always have done.'

'You must be potty.'

'I've been trying hard to think back to the first-year images,' says Jules. 'Those sweet little kids, sweet little faces. You just can't believe what's happened to everyone.'

'And to you,' says Raffy. 'Most of all.'

'That's what I mean,' says Jules. 'I wish we had taken a video of this evening five years ago. Look at Matt. Remember him in 1 G? He looked like a choir boy.'

Matt is now an hairy person, a Heavy Metaller, with hair down to there, who hardly speaks. He lives only for his guitar and magic mushrooms, though for his actual living, no one is sure where he does that.

'And what about Vinny?' continues Jules. 'I can see him now in his blazer, with his mum brushing his hair at the school gate on the first day.'

Vinny now has no hair, having had it all shaved off, the better to reveal the Union Jack tattoo on his forehead. He is now the school's prime yob, general bully and all-round hooligan, just as Matt is the token hippy.

'I keep thinking that inside each of them,

there still lurks the innocent little first-year,' says Jules.

'I'm surprised they're here,' says Raffy.

'They've been forced to come. They could get chucked out, otherwise. Lionel has done a three-line whip.'

Both Matt and Vinny are doing a one-year CPVE course, which stands for Certificate of Pre-Vocational Education. Mainly because they can't think of anything else to do. Better than working. Or even not working. About half the lower sixth are doing this course. Raffy and Jules, along with their old and bestest friends Sam, Ella, Kirsty, Colette and Dim, and their new friends Toby and Taz, are all doing A level courses, being brain boxes.

'Any sign of Taz?' says Raffy, staring around hopefully. They have decided Taz is a member of their group as she shares several lessons with them, but she seems hardly aware of it, remaining beautiful and exotic and aloof. She has only recently joined the sixth form, but is so far of it, rather than in it. Raffy has tried hard to force himself upon her, metaphorically at least, but with little success.

'Oh well,' says Raffy, draining his glass. 'Might as well go and give them the benefit of my wit and wisdom.'

'And my outfit,' says Jules. 'All the staff must be desperate by now to see it close up.'

Jules switches on his cap radio, then switches on himself. Raffy lingers for a second to drain Jules's glass. Then they both join the throng.

Sociology table, main hall

Mr Grott, Head of Sociology, is sitting, head in hand, listening, a tired but superior smile on his face. Opposite him sits Sam, not listening at all, looking round the hall and making grotesque faces when he catches the eye of any of his friends. Beside Sam sits his father, trying hard to concentrate. He is finding that all the loud conversations and arguments which are assaulting his ears on every side, plus the complicated jargon and details being thrown at him, have resulted in the most awful headache.

Sociology was meant for his wife, according to the battle plan, but she has decided he too should be present, to hear whatever it is they are going to hear. Sam's father wishes he'd taken a break and tried some of the PTA wine, though he knows that would have given him gut rot. To go with his splitting headache.

On Sam's other side sits his mother. She is the one talking. And the one Mr Grott is listening to.

'So what about Oxbridge?' she says.

Sam groans, wanting the floor to open up and swallow him.

'What about it, Mrs Graham?' asks Mr Grott.

'Well, in the fifth year, several teachers did say that Sam was capable of Oxford. His grandfather would so like him to go to his old college. I know his GCSE results were not all that brilliant –' she gives a little, steely glance at Sam, who now switches his furious face to the ceiling, hoping it will fall in, ' – but that was his own fault, too many distractions.'

'We'll have to see,' says Mr Grott, 'how he progresses.'

'Till when?' asks Mrs Graham.

'Oh, there's no panic,' says Mr Grott, offhand, putting his feet on the table to show off his new trainers.

'When have the UCCA forms got to be in?' asks Mrs Graham.

'Sam has got almost a year,' says Mr Grott, wearily, pointedly putting the stress on Sam's name, as of course it is Sam's concern, his decision, not his parents'. 'Around this time next year,' he continues, 'that's the time he can make up his mind. Oxbridge applications have to be in by 15 October, and the other universities by 15 December, unless they change the rules, which is always likely.'

'But will he have a chance?' persists Mrs Graham. 'I mean, is it worth his while to even think about it? I just want to know the position.'

'Well,' says Mr Grott, even more wearily, pulling up his white socks slowly, one at a time. 'As far as Sociology is concerned, little chance, I'm afraid. I don't expect, on his present showing, that he will get an A.'

'I see,' says Mrs Graham, tightly. 'Very kind of you to be so direct and honest. I'm obliged to you. Thanks for giving so much of your time.'

'A pleasure,' says Mr Grott.

Sam is already creeping away, looking for a hole

to climb into, followed by his mother and father. There is a scramble as another set of parents make a grab for the vacated chairs, arguing with another couple who maintain they were next, look, they have a timetable.

'I never liked him,' says Mrs Graham to her husband. 'I always distrust any adult over twenty-five who wears an earring.'

'Huh,' says Mr Graham. 'Earring? I didn't notice that.'

'You wouldn't,' says Mrs Graham.

The Maths table

Dim and his mother are sitting opposite one of the Maths teachers, Ms Upchart. She has been going through all Dim's cards and marks, pointing out his good points, which are many.

'So I really think you should think about Oxford,' says Ms Upchart.

'This is football team, innit?' says Dim's mother. These are the first words she has spoken so far. Football is a great talking point in their house, as Dim is captain of the school soccer team.

'Why not,' laughs Ms Upchart. 'I'm sure your clever son could manage both. Football could be a help, depending on which college he applies for. They are looking for good all-rounders these days, especially those from a comprehensive.'

Dim's mother nods. She now knows what a comprehensive is. Lots of tables in a big hall and a great deal of talking, all very different from the remote village school she went to.

'I dunno,' says Dim. 'I don't wanna go to that sort of snob place. I fancy Manchester.'

'Nothing wrong with Manchester,' says Ms Upchart. 'But there's no hurry. You can start going round various places next term and see what you think. Lots of them have open days.'

'Do they pay for you to go?' asks Dim.

Ms Upchart laughs again.

'I'm not going nowhere,' says Dim, 'if I gotta pay.'

'There will probably be special buses going to some places,' says Ms Upchart. 'So that would help your financial situation, hmm, Dmitri?'

'Huh,' says Dim.

Ms Upchart laughs again. For some reason, she has always found Dim funny. Now that she has seen his mother for the first time, she feels even more warmly towards him.

The English table

Colette is furious that she has been placed on the list to be seen by the Head of English, Mrs Batty, a teacher she has never liked and one who hardly knows her anyway.

'I wish I had done English at university . . .' says Colette's mother. Colette groans. Mrs Batty looks at her watch. '. . . I did a General Arts degree, BA, but really, I should have done English.'

Mrs Batty looks down her notes, turns over her register, checks a few names and figures.

'I've regretted it really, ever since,' continues

Colette's mother. 'I was so very good at English . . .'

'The result of your last test, Colette,' says Mrs Batty, breaking in.

'Yes,' says Colette, vacantly.

'It was appalling,' says Mrs Batty.

'So what?' says Colette, chewing gum. 'Not my fault. That stupid man gave us stuff we'd never done.'

'Colette!' says her mother. 'Don't use that word about any teacher. And stop chewing.'

'Will if I want,' says Colette. 'It's true. It was some crappy poem by Wordsworth we'd never done before.'

'It was an Unseen,' says Mrs Batty. 'That is the point of it.'

'Stupid point, if you ask me,' says Colette. She catches sight of Ella at the next table and gives her best curled-lip, disdainful sneer.

'As for *Vanity Fair*,' continues Mrs Batty, referring to the novel which she is teaching Colette's class, 'I am sick and tired of you handing in such short essays.'

'Oh come on,' says Colette, rising to the bait, feeling very self-righteous and hard-done-by. 'That is unfair.'

From her folder, Mrs Batty pulls out Colette's last essay, two pages of it, covered with red marks, and lays it on the table.

'So?' says Colette.

'Look at it,' says Mrs Batty.

'Well if you hadn't messed it up with your rotten scribbles, it would look very neat.'

'I'm not talking about neatness. I am talking firstly about content, and then length.'

'Whajamean?' explodes Colette. 'I specifically come and asked you, don't say you've forgotten, at the end of the lesson. I said how much to write and you says two pages. Is that right or is that right?'

'I said *at least* two pages,' says Mrs Batty. 'Just look at them.'

Colette has indeed handed in two pages, but page two consists of only one line.

'Yeah, that was some effort,' says Colette, laughing at her own uselessness, 'getting over the page.' She turns to her mother, hoping she will see the joke and join in against the teacher, but her mother is furious.

'I don't know what's happened to her recently,' says her mother.

'Well, what are we going to do about it?' growls Mrs Batty, looking hard at Colette's mother. 'This has become serious I'm afraid, Mrs Cavendish, er Ms Cavendish.'

Mrs Batty has for a moment forgotten how to address Colette's mother. At the back of her mind, she knows there is no husband, but can't remember if both Colette and her mother have the same surname.

'Call me Gloria,' simpers Colette's mother.

This makes Colette really mad, watching her mother creep to Mrs Batty and take her side, not listening to her daughter's point of view.

'It's just not good enough,' says Mrs Batty,

pushing the offending essay away as if it is contaminated.

'Well, nobody helps you in this place,' says Colette. 'We just get left, no one cares. How do I know what to do?'

'You can't expect to be spoonfed for ever, Colette,' says Mrs Batty. 'All that has finished. In the sixth form we expect a large degree of self-motivation, especially from students hoping to take A level exams.'

'Yes, I am very pleased about that,' begins Colette's mother.

'Well, I wouldn't bank on it,' says Mrs Batty.

'Whajamean?' says Colette, rudely but also slightly fearfully.

'Well, if the standard of her essays gets no better between now and Christmas, if she continues to do no outside reading whatsoever, if she still shows such little interest in English, and if she is determined to try and get away with only the absolute minimum, then I'm afraid I will recommend to Mr Witting that Colette gives up the A level course and is transferred to a CPVE course.'

Colette's mother looks horrified. She is not quite sure what a CPVE is, but realizes it can't lead to a university place. All three sit looking at each other, meaningfully. Colette eventually turns away, hoping to catch someone's eye, but all her friends seem to be exchanging serious, meaningful looks with somebody else.

'You never know,' says Mrs Batty. 'That might suit Colette very well. You could find that a simple pre-vocational course will be best for her in the long run. And for everyone concerned.'

Mrs Batty looks up and over Colette's mother's head, glancing at the queue behind, giving a nod to indicate that she is ready for the next customer, the next victim.

'She's just lazy,' says Colette's mother, desperately. 'That's all it is. I know. Pure laziness.'

Colette is on her feet, almost in tears, but the strength of her fury is keeping them back. She rushes through the hall, leaving her mother behind, and runs down the corridors and out of school.

Jules: man about the Heath

EPISODE 3

Next morning, Hampstead Heath

Jules has just left home and is jogging to school, taking a long way round as he suddenly feels inspired to get fit. There are, however, two obstacles in the way, stopping him from an all-out, whole-hearted attempt to become a serious jogger.

'Oh God, not again!' he exclaims, suddenly stopping. He then dances up and down on one leg.

His cry startles two Russian women, carrying massive shopping bags. They have just left their official residence, beside the Heath, and are heading for a dawn swoop on the capitalist pleasures of Kentish Town, namely Sainsbury's. They cease their chattering when they hear Jules's exclamation and pass him in silence. Naturally, they do not stop to enquire if they can help, nor do they smile or show any signs of noticing him. Jules is used to this. He knows the ways of the Russian trade and diplomatic families who live beside Hampstead Heath. They have been trained never to react.

'Bloody dog shit,' shouts Jules.

The two women turn round, exchange looks, then hurry on.

'Not you, madam,' says Jules. *'Do svidanya.'* He does not speak Russian but as a linguist, with an A in GCSE French and a B in German, he prides himself on knowing a few words of all the major languages, even if it's only hello and goodbye.

Jules stops beside one of the ponds. He finds a stick and manages to scrape the offending excrement off the soles of his new Reebok trainers, top of the line, only £49.

'Why am I jogging anyway,' he says to himself. 'No one can see me.' That's his second objection to jogging on the Heath. The lack of any suitable audience.

He carefully cleans both shoes on some wet grass, then sets off again, slowly and leisurely, keeping an eye out just in case he meets any people. If he does, he is ready to begin his Chariots of Fire jubilatory jog. The only person he passes is a middle-aged man with a moustache and a pair of binoculars who is taking a golden retriever for a walk. He hears the man shouting for the dog, calling the name 'Crumble', which Jules considers the most ridiculous name he has ever heard.

Jules leaves the Heath, getting ready to break into

a trot, knowing he is bound to start meeting people he knows pretty soon.

'Ouch, what was that?' he shouts. He has been banged into by a figure rushing out from behind a hedge.

'Hey, that hurt!' says Jules. He checks his trainers for any dirty marks, his tracksuit for any splashes, and then his baseball radio cap for any interference with the pirate station he has carefully tuned into.

'Oh sorry, man,' grunts the figure, half-hidden by his long red hair.

'Matt!' says Jules. 'What the hell are you doing?'

'I live here, man,' says Matt.

Jules looks over the hedge, which is completely overgrown, into an even more overgrown garden. Behind it there is a large house, with all its windows boarded up and the front door barricaded.

'You live there?' says Jules.

'Yeah,' says Matt. 'For the moment.'

'Oh God, look,' says Jules.

Matt stares back at the house, presuming Jules has seen someone or something at the window.

'My socks!' says Jules. 'They're ruined. It's like a farmyard round here.'

'Sorry, man,' says Matt. 'Do you wanna come in and wash them? I think we've got running water today.' He turns back towards the house and Jules follows him.

'It's amazing,' says Jules. 'It's so sort of Gothic.'

'No, I think it's Victorian,' says Matt.

They get to the front door and Matt bangs on it

four times, in a rhythmic pattern. Then he does it again.

'Perhaps nobody's in,' says Jules.

'Nah,' says Matt. 'The King's in. I know. He'll be watching.' He bangs again. This time there is shouting from inside.

'No pigs,' shouts a voice. 'I can smell the stink from here.'

Jules looks at Matt for an explanation, then he glances down at his socks.

'I think he could be right about the smell,' says Jules, examining his socks. 'The dirty marks aren't your fault. It's those dogs on the Heath.'

'You sleep out there, do you?' says Matt.

'Come on,' says Jules. 'We'll be late for school. I'll buy another pair on the way.'

Later, in the common room

Raffy is talking about the parents' evening, telling everyone who will listen, and those who won't, what the staff said to him last night. 'In a word,' he says, 'magic. Everyone of them said the same. They're all amazed, knocked out, that one person can be so good at everything, and is also handsome and witty and sexy.'

'Oh, so you're talking about me now, are you?' says Jules. 'Just one thing you missed out. Stylish. Which is something you are never going to be, Raphael old fruit.'

'Who would want to be that?' asks Raffy. 'Waste of energy, waste of money, waste of bonking time, going and buying stupid clothes.'

'Hey, Jules,' says Ella. 'You didn't see Mrs Batty last night. She was looking for you.'

'Darling,' says Jules, 'I haven't got time to see everyone. If they get behind, that's their own fault. What I'm doing for the next parents' evening is arranging my own timetable, on a fan, so that they can come and see me at set times.'

Colette and Kirsty laugh, enjoying the image, which encourages Jules to elaborate further. 'Now, where shall I give my audience?' he says. 'I think the Savoy Grill perhaps, over cocktails beside the piano, or possibly at the bar at Dingwalls, depending on my mood and what's on. I'll send little cards to all the staff, "Jules will be At Home" –'

'Oh shurrup, you fairy,' says a loud voice. In a far corner, Vinny and some of his cronies are having a chair-lifting competition, taking turns to pick up a wooden chair by the leg using one hand.

In the lower years, especially the third and fourth, Jules had to put up with a lot of such remarks, but his quick wit usually helped him out of trouble, or his friends came to his assistance. Now, in the sixth, there are few people who ever make such personal comments. Several people glare at Vinny, but Jules has chosen to ignore him. The chatting starts again, till there is a loud crash from Vinny's end of the common room. In celebrating lifting the chair higher than anyone else, Vinny has deliberately let it fall to the floor. It collapses in a heap on the carpet, two legs broken.

The door opens and in comes Mr Witting. His office is next door to the common room, but he tries never to intrude unless absolutely necessary. He stares at the broken chair.

'Who did that?' asks Mr Witting.

No one replies, but most people are staring in Vinny's direction.

'I just sat on it,' says Vinny, 'and it broke.'

'You did what?' says Mr Witting, coldly, looking at the damage.

'I told you,' repeats Vinny insolently. 'It broke when I sat on it.'

Mr Witting has had several reports already about Vinny's behaviour in the sixth form, so he doesn't believe this feeble excuse. But he continues glaring, as if waiting for Vinny to commit another offence or possibly go mad, tell the truth for once and admit his guilt.

'Let's go,' says Vinny, standing up, speaking to his henchmen. 'This place is dead.'

'Yeah, let's go and make something happen,' says one of his cronies.

'Yeah, man,' says Vinny, 'let's go and hassle someone.' He says this provocatively, smirking, announcing it as a half-joke, though everyone takes it as a whole truth and waits for Mr Witting to react.

'Yes,' says Jules, 'there must be some first years out there you can really hassle.'

Vinny expected to have the last word and leave the common room on his terms, surrounded by his gang. There are laughs all round at Jules's remark, much to Vinny's obvious displeasure.

The common room relaxes once Vinny and Co. have gone. Mr Witting looks round, searching out a few faces. 'The bell has gone, Raphael,' he says. 'I'm pretty sure you do have a lesson.'

'Oh, sorry sir,' says Raffy, getting up. 'Awfully sorry. Just going.'

'And you, Kirsty, shouldn't you be in the Art room?'

She too gets up. Mr Witting is now treating them all like juveniles, indicating that some of them obviously cannot behave like adults.

As Mr Witting leaves the common room, he turns to Jules. 'Could I have a word with you?' he says. 'In ten minutes.'

Mr Witting's office

Mr Witting and his deputy, Miss Kling, are poring over a computer print-out, looking very perplexed. Jules, who has arrived on time, is standing in a corner by the door of Mr Witting's overcrowded office, looking cool and relaxed. There is a stacking chair he can sit on, but he prefers to stand and keep his clothes uncreased. Anyway, the chair looks a bit dusty, as do so many of the files, boxes and pigeon holes in Mr Witting's room.

'I think we put in the wrong code,' says Mr Witting. 'Last year we had a different reference for some of the Certificate of Pre-Vocational Education courses. That could explain it.'

There has been a sudden spate of lower-sixth people coming in, saying their timetable does not make sense. Some of the new CPVE classes on Information Technology, TV and the Media, which are supposed to have come onstream by now, have not registered on the computer. They take place outside school at other institutions, which has added to the confusion.

'We'll have to program it again,' groans Mr Witting.

Jules looks at his watch, then turns on his radio cap, swaying gently to a reggae beat. Outside the office, through the glass wall, he can see three other lower sixth formers, all waiting. Jules smiles and blows kisses at them. At least he has got inside. So boring, having to stand outside and queue with the rabble. He picks out some old university prospectuses from a box and starts studying them. He is not looking at the words but the photographs, trying to decide which university appears to have the best-dressed students.

'Hey, this looks good,' he mutters. 'Red gowns, really chic. I could go for that.' He turns over and finds the prospectus is for St Andrews University, in Scotland. 'That's neat as well. From one St Andrews to another St Andrews.'

Jules is so busy looking at the photographs, preoccupied with the styles, that he fails to stop an upper-sixth girl from bursting in. She is small with very short hair and looks very determined.

'Hey, I've been trying to see you,' she says, going straight up to Mr Witting's desk, looking as if she is going to strangle him. He reacts by throwing a book at her. Not quite at her, though it does slide off the table at her feet, but in her general direction.

'There's my diary,' says Mr Witting. 'Find a gap,

fill in your name, then get out. You can see I'm busy.'

The girl inserts her name in his diary, booking five minutes from the rest of his life, then she leaves.

Mr Witting eventually resolves the computer problem and turns towards Jules when Ms Kling has departed. Jules smiles. He has been getting ready a smart comment about the girl. 'That was your last year's diary,' says Jules. 'Good trick, huh.'

'Sit down,' says Mr Witting, curtly.

Jules looks carefully around, then lightly dusts the stacking chair before lowering his precious body with its precious cargo into it.

'You could do a great deal better, you know,' says Mr Witting.

'Impossible,' says Jules.

'Such as coming to see me last night,' says Mr Witting. 'I had you on my list but you never turned up. Yet I saw you there, drinking.'

'That was a mistake,' says Jules.

'Good,' says Mr Witting, looking at some notes on his desk.

'Yes, it tasted like turpentine. I should have stuck to the instant coffee. It only tastes of washing-up water, so it's not too harmful for the old insides.'

Mr Witting manages a wintery smile. 'You know, Jules, you could be really good. In fact you could excel. You are quick, with great originality and flair, but you are selling yourself short.'

'I may be short, but I am fit,' says Jules. 'On the old Heath first thing this morning, jogging away . . .'

'That's the sort of thing I mean,' says Mr Witting.

'You are too preoccupied with making smart remarks. You don't take enough things seriously.'

Jules puts on his serious face.

'You managed easily enough in the lower years,
with some native wit and speed, and your GCSE
results were good. But for A levels there has to be a
bit of backbone, some real work done. Not only
done, but shown to be done. It's no good being
flippant in your essays, showing off, just to amuse
the markers by being one step ahead of them. They
don't all appreciate that. They don't need your
wisecracks, they want content, proof that you know
things.'

'Are you saying I'm lazy?'

'Not lazy,' says Mr Witting, 'facetious. You are
too concerned with your image.'

Jules stretches his legs, pulls up his new white
socks, examines his trainers.

'If you put as much effort and thought into your
work as you do into your appearance, then with your
talent, there is nothing you wouldn't be able to
achieve.'

'Who says I want to achieve anything?' replies
Jules, getting up. 'What if my talent is to amuse?'

'Look, I haven't got time to discuss this any more.
All I'm saying is, change some of your ways before
your ways change you.'

'That's pretty smart,' says Jules. 'I'll use that.'

Mr Witting can be heard sighing as Jules leaves
his office. But there is also the trace of a smile on his
face as he goes back to the computer print-outs.

Colette: heart's desire

EPISODE 4

Camden Town, Saturday morning

Colette is walking very quickly, determined not to be distracted. She slows down going past the stalls at Camden Lock, but decides not to stop. 'Just for the tourists,' she thinks. 'Though I could have a look at Sam's stall, see what he's got today.'

It is not exactly Sam's stall, but his father's, made up of leftovers from his various dopey collections. Sometimes Kirsty looks after the stall, but she and Ella are weight-training this morning. Colette used to join them, but has now given up all hope of ever having an athletic, sylph-like figure.

'No, it's all rubbish. I'm fed up with second-hand stuff anyway. That's all I've ever had in my whole life.' She passes on, weaving in and out of the crowded pavements, dodging the litter and junk and impromptu stalls, the fast-food tables, the fast-talking dealers. The voices in her ears seem to be all

Scandinavian today. A whole load of them must have arrived for the weekend, to stock up on British junk.

Colette feels hungry with all the smells, but manages not to be tempted. Hot pancakes dripping with sugar and chocolate sauce might be different, but dodgy-looking vege burgers or pitta bread filled with debris she finds easy to resist. Anyway, she hasn't got money to spare for such minor fripperies. Not when she has set her heart on a major frippery.

She steps carefully at Camden Town tube station, avoiding the druggies and the dossers, the tramps and the trollops, but recognizes two thirteen-year-olds from school. Their eyes are bright and shiny with innocence, despite their heavily rouged cheeks, deliberately torn tights and obscenely short skirts.

'Gawd, takes me back,' thinks Colette. 'The hours I spent there, waiting for people, waiting for things to happen. But nothing ever did, well hardly ever did. I feel a hundred, just looking at them. If only I knew then what I know now. Remind me, what do I know now? Answer: not a lot.

'The thing about being thirteen is that you don't know what you don't know. You think you know the lot, that you are discovering *it* all by yourself, the first discoverer ever, that you've got there before anyone else. So you go mad, or some folks do.

'Now where was that party where someone smashed up all the furniture? Then threw the contents of the fridge at every wall? Somewhere in

Hampstead. I'll ask Raffy. He did most of the throwing. Then the throwing-up. Wish I could have a party. Never had one ever. That stupid old woman. And her stupid boyfriends. When I have my own house I'll have all my friends in, all the time. "When I have my own house," what a laff. I'll never have anything in life, no job, and certainly no house, not at this rate.'

Colette slows her step and her brain, going down a few gears, deliberately relaxing herself. After all, what she is heading for might already have gone. She stops and waits outside the Kentucky Fried Chicken emporium. She breathes in and flexes her muscles, not to savour the delicate gourmet smells but to get her body ready, just in case it is about to be transformed.

'Fat chance,' she thinks.

She decides she is at last ready to make a dash for the top, a final assault on the summit. Looking around, she takes another deep breath, then rushes like a wild thing, or a child in a playground, just let out of school. It is only a dash of five metres to the next shop, but all the way she is praying that *it* will still be there.

It still sits in the corner of the shop window. It's a perfectly ordinary clothes shop and Jules would be appalled that anyone could even look in such a window. Her eyes take in the brown leather jacket. Nothing fancy, nothing outlandish, not even very fashionable, but Colette has got it into her head that this brown leather jacket will change her life, or at least her winter. She has been looking for weeks in supposedly more desirable shops, the places most of her friends frequent, such as Top Shop, Jigsaw, Warehouse, and even Miss Selfridge. None of them has got quite this jacket, the one this shop has in its window. Colette is not even sure if the shop has a name, or just a street number.

'Still £79.99,' she says to herself. 'Why don't they have a sale and reduce it just a little, rotten sods.' There are still three weeks to go before the next part of her allowance is due. Till then, she has nothing. Except for £19.50 in her Barclays Supersavers account which she has had there for years, almost as a talisman, hoping it might miraculously grow over-night into real money, such as £79.99.

It is the third Saturday morning she has made this trip just to ogle at the window. The first two visits she tried the jacket on; now she feels it would be too pathetic to do so again. 'Gawd,' she moans, turning away. 'I can't bear it. Why doesn't it get sold? That would solve everything.'

Colette sets off home, slowly, looking now in every window, inspecting every stall, every pave-ment. 'Well it's put the morning in. Pretty exciting, for a Saturday. Mind you, not like the third-form years. Yes, those were the days. All gone now. Ah well, roll on me pension . . .'

Saturday evening, Colette's flat

The candles are already lit, the freshly ironed nap-kins laid out, the Beaujolais is opened, the French bread all cut up, the battered studio couch covered with an amusing ethnic rug to hide the stain. In turn, the ethnic rug is covered with an even more amusing crochet blanket, to hide the ethnic holes. Even the paper lampshade has been dusted.

'Hmm,' says Colette's mother. 'That was a mistake. Look at it. Doesn't look very safe. I said dust it, not decimate it.'

'Misuse of the word "decimate",' says Colette. 'We had that in English yesterday.'

'Oh, so you *are* doing some work now. Thank goodness for that.'

'I will ignore that remark, pig,' says Colette. 'Yes, "decimate" is from the Latin and means to reduce by a tenth, but people will use it as if it means kill off or destroy completely.'

'I just can't believe I did Latin,' says Colette's mother. 'But we had to, in my day, to get into any reasonable sort of university.'

'Oh Gawd, why did I mention it,' groans Colette. She climbs on the table to examine the paper lampshade which is now hanging loosely from the central light.

'Don't touch it!' shouts her mother.

Too late. The lampshade has come away in Colette's hands.

'It's like a dead body,' says Colette, flicking the bits of hanging wire and tattered paper, watching them swing back and forward, as grime and dust fall on the clean tablecloth and into the waiting, expectant glasses.

'Oh do shut up, Colette,' says her mother.

'The skull of an ancient Egyptian, turned into papyrus. Oooh. Spoooooooky . . .'

'I think you have a morbid sense of humour, child.'

'I love dust and dirt,' says Colette. 'I love seeing what they can do. Just think Mother, in only three years this lampshade has been eaten away, destroyed by particles in the air. Think of what they're doing to our bodies. We are disintegrating, even as we speak . . .'

'Do be quiet and go and get a brush and clear up the mess.'

'Plus of course the smoke,' says Colette. 'Your smoke. You are the one who has been killing us.'

'You know I've stopped.'

'Yeah, but the damage has been done. If I get lung cancer in the years to come it will be your fault, making me breathe your smoke when I was a baby.'

'Are you going out or not?' says her mother, going to fetch the pan and brush.

'No, I think I'll just stay in. Sit here and watch the orgy.'

'That's enough of that,' says her mother. She clears the debris away, then takes a pink bulb out of the standard lamp beside the couch and swaps it with the one in the bare overhead light.

'How do you think that looks, Colette?' she asks.

'You look horrible,' says Colette, sitting down and reading *City Limits*.

'I didn't ask you about my clothes.'

All afternoon, Colette's mother has fussed and fretted. She has changed four times and is now wearing a peasant-girl long floral skirt, very sixties, and a Wallis blouse, very seventies. She has finally made an executive decision to dress her age, not hide it. *City Limits* has been bought specially, to show she is still young in her heart and young in her interests, outlook and, dare one say it, passions. Colette certainly can't. The very thought sickens her.

'What about a high chair?' says Colette. She says it in an American accent, stressing the 'high', as in high school.

'What?' says her mother, worrying that she might have forgotten something.

'And his bib and his feeding cup, and where will you put his pushchair, and let's hope he brings a spare nappy.'

'That's enough of that.'

'Well he is only thirteen,' says Colette.

'Thirty, actually,' says her mother.

'What a lie,' says Colette. 'You told me he said he remembered me from school. So if that's true, and let's say I was in the first year when he was just leaving, in the sixth form to give him the benefit of the doubt, then let me see, he can't be any more than, hold on, he can't be more than, at the most, twenty-five. So you are sussed, doubled sussed.'

'Oh do be quiet. I can't remember what he said.'

'No wonder, at your age.'

'Are you going or not?' asks her mother.

'No, I'm staying in. It's my chance to meet him. You can say I'm the au pair, or your little sister. Or the maid. I'll wear frilly knickers and speak French. But I promise not to get off with him. After all, I'm not a baby snatcher, unlike some people.'

'Okay then,' says her mother, going to the fridge. She opens it, takes out a cellophane-covered packet from the back and produces an old travel wallet announcing 'Caribbean Connections'. Out of it she takes a ten-pound note which she hands to Colette.

'Bribery, bribery,' says Colette, getting up. 'All is bribery. But it's not my fault. I haven't got a penny, have I.'

She gives her mother a kiss. 'Have a nice meal,' she says. 'And don't worry, I won't be too early home.'

The pub, later the same evening

Colette and Kirsty are sitting up at the bar of the Cow and Bull, each supping half a pint of bitter paid for by Kirsty. Colette is keeping quiet about her massive windfall.

'This is bleedin' pathetic,' says Colette. 'What we gonna do?'

'Dunno.'

'Get lost, rat face,' says Kirsty.

'Excuse me,' says Colette.

'Not you, love,' says Kirsty. 'Don't look round now; Vinny has arrived. He's coming this way.'

They both turn their backs, ignoring Vinny when he comes over and tries to talk them, but he soon moves on, heading for the lavatory.

'Anything else, darlings?' says Neville, the manager. 'Any special treats you'd like me to concoct, hmm?'

'Up your bum,' says Colette. They both swivel round again, this time with their backs to the bar.

'Where the hell are they?' says Kirsty. 'I'm fed up being hassled. Let's hire a video and go to your place.'

'Can't,' says Colette. 'Impossible.' She has no wish to go into details.

'Well we can't go to my dump,' says Kirsty. 'So that's out.'

'I hate this pub,' says Colette.

'I hate all pubs,' says Kirsty.

'You're full of hate tonight, girls,' says Neville.

'Mostly of you,' says Kirsty.

The bar door opens and in comes Dim, at long last. He was due almost an hour ago.

'About bloody time,' says Colette.

'Where the hell is Raffy?' Kirsty asks.

'Dunno,' says Dim. 'I thought he'd be with you.'

For a moment Dim contemplates giving them a kiss each, just a quick peck in the sixth-form manner, as Raffy and Jules would do and Sam too. Even Toby is assuming most of such sixth-form form and fashions. But Dim still feels kissing is too arty, at least too much 'arts sixth', too phoney for him as a realist and a scientist.

'Right,' says Dim. 'Who's gonna buy me a drink?'

'On your bike,' says Kirsty. 'You're loaded.'

'Yeah,' says Dim, 'but it's all invested. Can't touch it.'

'Okay then,' says Colette, sighing. 'It is my turn.' She takes out her ten-pound note. Kirsty gives an exaggerated cry of disbelief. Dim holds the note up to the light to test it's genuine. As he does so, a hand appears over his shoulder and grabs it from him.

For a moment, Colette and Kirsty fear it might be Vinny stealing it, or perhaps Neville playing silly buggers. Then loud, raucous laughter gives the game away.

'Gotcha!' exclaims Raffy.

'Hey, hold on,' says Dim.

'Do you mind!' says Colette.

'What will it be, ladies?' leers Neville, seeing the ten-pound note being flashed around.

'Nothing at all, squire,' says Raffy, putting an arm round each of the girls and pulling them off their stools. 'Follow me, folks,' he says. 'We'll need that tenner. Be useful to buy a few bottles.'

'What's happening, Raffy?' squeals Kirsty, putting on the excitement.

'Yes, do tell,' says Colette, affecting her posh voice.

'We're going to an orgy, that's all,' says Raffy.

'Where?' says Dim, ever practical.

'I've found an empty house. Follow me . . .'

Kirsty: out on the town

EPISODE 5

Saturday evening, even later

Raffy is leading the way down various streets, taking short cuts down alleys, looking mysterious but also very pleased with himself. Dim isn't convinced. Kirsty and Colette, arm in arm, are also cynical, convinced this is one of Raffy's stupid jokes but amused and intrigued at the thought that something might be about to happen.

'Better than the rotten pub,' says Colette.

'Anything's better than that,' Kirsty agrees.

'I hope I'll get my reward from you two young ladies, I mean women,' says Raffy.

'Get lost,' says Colette.

'No chance,' says Kirsty. They both snigger.

'Oh come on. I've saved you from a fate worse than death,' says Raffy.

'Oh yeah, what's that?' says Kirsty.

'Having nothing to do on a Saturday night,' says Raffy. 'Do you realize, in the whole universe there are millions and billions of people praying this very moment for something to do, just anything. All because it's Saturday night.'

'What's he on about?' says Kirsty.

'He's gone loony,' says Colette.

'You got it,' says Raffy. 'Loony because of the lunar influence. At this precise moment, trillions of people round the globe are looking up at that same moon – see, the one up there – and thinking the same thoughts. All wishing they had Raffy in their life, to whisk them off somewhere exciting. Just because it's Saturday night. And they all hope it's gonna be all right.'

'Not true,' says Dim. 'Not trillions. It's only Saturday night here, on this latitude. In Brisbane or Sydney, Shanghai or Bangkok, it's Sunday morning. In San Francisco or Vancouver, it's still only Saturday morning.'

'Bloody pedant,' says Raffy. 'You scientists are all the same. You want to take the fun out of life and just leave in the facts. Well, yous are lucky anyway, girls, yous are with me. It's Saturday night. It *will be all right!*' He jumps up and down, punching the air, singing and dancing.

'Look, stop messing about,' says Kirsty. 'Where we going?'

'Keep your hair on,' says Raffy. 'And your

clothes. For the moment; I'll be taking both of them off later.'

'On your bike,' says Kirsty.

'Hey, that's a position I haven't tried,' says Raffy. 'We'll have a go tonight. You can come for a ride with me.'

'We're just going round in circles, you wally,' says Colette.

'Quick, down here,' shouts Raffy, suddenly crouching as he approaches a street corner, putting his finger to his mouth. 'Get beside this wall,' he hisses. 'Col, Kirst, Dim. At once. If they find us, deny everything. This might be pretty hairy . . .'

'What a fool he is,' says Kirsty. 'Come on, Col, let's go home.'

Raffy gets up, looks back down the street, then dashes ahead round the corner and disappears. The others stop, sigh and make faces, all refusing to smile, then slowly they walk forward. There is no sign of Raffy. They look around, puzzled, until he suddenly reappears, staggering out of an off licence carrying several cans of beer.

'If that's my bloody money, you pig –' says Colette.

'Course it is,' says Raffy. 'Plus a bit of my own. In fact you owe me 10p, but I'll let you off.' He looks at his watch, then becomes serious at last. 'Right, the orgy is now about to begin. Sorry about that. I just wanted to put in fifteen minutes, so we didn't arrive too early.'

Raffy leads the way, taking a right and a left, going down a street which they instantly recognize.

'So it is a joke after all,' says Kirsty.

'No it's not,' says Raffy. 'Look, I'll press the bell, then we'll all stand round the side so we can't be seen. Come on, do what I say.'

He presses the bell, checks his watch again, looks up at the top floor where he can see a light, then he pushes everyone to the side of the door. The door opens, but only a few feet, and a face looks out. It is Sam. Raffy bounds forward, forces the door wide open and dashes in, followed by Dim.

'Samuel, old son,' says Raffy. 'How kind of you to invite us. But we haven't come empty-handed. These are for you.'

'Oh Gawd,' says Sam. 'I thought it was me dad coming back.'

'No chance,' says Raffy. 'I've checked. Won't be back for hours. This way, girls. It's your Big Night . . .'

Sam's room

Ella is sitting on Sam's bed, where until a few moments ago she was settled very happily, listening to sweet music and sharing sweet nothings with Sam. Now she is absolutely furious about what has happened.

'Ring the police, Sam,' she says. 'Say you've got burglars, which is what Raffy is. An uninvited intruder.'

'Don't be like that, Ella,' says Raffy. 'You should take pity on us. We're the Saturday Night Homeless, the displaced persons. You wouldn't want us to spend another Saturday night in hell, would you?

I've had enough for ever of Camden Town tube station.' He beams, pleased that his strategy has worked, pleased with his smart remarks, looking round at Dim, Colette and Kirsty for approval.

'Don't push it, Raf,' says Kirsty.

'But it's true,' says Raffy. 'I can't have anybody in my place, ever, can I? Nor can Kirsty or Dim. You know that. And Colette can hardly manage it either, certainly not tonight. You've got to feel sorry for us.'

'Who's been talking to you, Raffy?' asks Colette.

'I have my spies,' says Raffy, opening one of the cans of beer he has just given Sam.

'How did you find out about, you know, here?' asks Kirsty, looking meaningfully at Ella, sulking on the bed, and Sam, fed-up and resigned.

'More spies,' says Raffy, taking a swig. 'Actually it was Toby. I rang him up, asked him what's he doing tonight, and he says he has to stay in and buttle. You what, I says. Come again Tobe, in English. I know I'm the cleverest, the quickest, the most multi-talented person in the whole sixth form, but hang about . . .'

Raffy pauses, waiting to be asked to continue, but nobody does so. 'All right, I'll tell you, peasants,' he goes on. 'His parents are giving this big posh booze party and Toby has to help pour out the wine. So naturally I asked if I could come, do some of the buttling for them, but he says no chance, it's for the geriatrics of the neighbourhood. So I says does that mean my gran is invited and he laughs and says no, but Sam's parents are.'

'So that's where they are,' says Sam.

'It started at nine,' says Raffy, checking his watch again. 'There's food at ten and a live jazz band at eleven, so by my reckoning there's no chance of them being back this side of midnight. By which time they'll be paralytic. So old-fashioned, the older generation. Don't you think? Do you remember when we used to go boozing, at about thirteen or fourteen. Just a phase, we gave it up for more stimulating pleasures. And we've got the next three hours at least to be really stimulated.'

'Not bad,' says Dim. 'Well sussed.'

'But how did you know only Ella and Sam would be here?' asks Colette.

'Sam told me,' says Raffy.

'What?' says Ella.

'I rang Sam, didn't I,' says Raffy. 'He says he's staying in tonight working on his essay, and other cobblers, so I thought bingo.'

'You pig,' says Ella.

'Quite right,' says Raffy, throwing himself on the bed beside Ella, who immediately gets up. 'So here I am, full of fun and ready to go – grunt, grunt, grunt.'

Sarah's bedroom, Sam's house

Dim and Colette are both sitting side by side on Sarah's bed. Sarah, Sam's fifteen-year-old sister, is staying the night with a friend. Dim is concentrating hard on some problem in his mind. Colette, looking suitably solemn and receptive, strokes his cheek to help his brainpower. But she can't keep up her serious, sensitive look for long, not without help. She sighs, then leans over and puts her hand under the bed, feeling around to see if there's anything interesting. She pulls out a Madonna poster.

'Worralaff, eh?' says Colette, imitating Cilla Black. 'So this is where she's hidden the secrets of her childhood. Worralass.'

'Huh,' says Dim.

'It's Sade on the wall and Madonna under the bed,' says Colette. 'That sums up her generation. I wonder what will be next.'

'Huh,' says Dim.

'What have you got under your bed, Dim?'

'Huh.'

'Oh I forgot,' says Colette. 'You haven't got a bed. You sleep on a shelf.'

'Shush,' says Dim.

'Sam and Ella can't hear us next door, he's got his music on. No need to shush me, you goof.'

'Huh.'

'So what you thinking about?' says Colette, lying down on the bed again and stroking Dim's leg. 'Hmm, what muscles.'

'Just working it out,' says Dim.

'That's good,' says Colette.

'You've been absolutely stupid,' says Dim.

'How come?' says Colette.

'Keeping your £19.50 in Barclays Supersavers all these years. It's only been paying 4.5 per cent. You should have transferred it to Barclays Plus savings account, which is for over-fourteens, and you get 5.25 per cent.'

'Oooh,' says Colette. 'So I might have bought my jacket by now.'

'But the best teenager bank account at the moment is the Midland's Number One. They're paying 6.75 per cent, last time I looked, and you get lots of freebies.'

'Oooh Dimmy, come on then, excite me.'

'Well, you get a project file, a pen, a sports bag, and a T-shirt. And I think – don't quote me on this, it could have changed – you can even get a camera.'

'Woweee,' says Colette. 'Life's good.'

'Then you can change your account the moment you've got the freebies. Spread it around, as I do, opening an account in different places. A fiver is often enough. I've had a free record from the TSB and a pocket calculator from the Nat West and lots of other stuff.'

'I haven't got enough to spread it around,' says Colette. 'I'm saving it all for you, Dimmy.' She moves her hand slowly up his leg.

'Seriously, Colette,' says Dim. 'It's no wonder you never have any money. You never save. You just spend all your allowance the moment it comes in.'

'Don't care,' says Colette, pouting.

'But you do care,' says Dim, 'because all you do is moan about money. We've all heard for weeks about this mad jacket you can't afford to buy.'

'So?'

'People who really don't care about money, don't care about buying things either,' says Dim.

'Oh Gawd, I haven't come here to be lectured,' says Colette. 'I came here to find a lecher – gerrit, Dimmy?' She lies back on the bed, stretching her legs, trying hard to appear provocative.

'It's not funny,' says Dim. 'You've got to get on top of money before it gets on top of you.'

'Oh goody, fun at last,' says Colette.

She rolls over and jumps on top of Dim. He continues to look serious for a while, but Colette soon has him smiling and laughing, relaxing at last . . .

Sam's bedroom

Ella is walking round the room, not speaking to Sam, abstractedly examining his possessions. 'Look, it wasn't my fault,' says Sam, sighing. He is lying on the bed, his hands behind his head, looking up at the ceiling.

'Didn't know you still liked Whitney Houston,' says Ella, flatly, coldly. Showing she is still not in a good mood, but at least no longer sulking in silence.

'I couldn't help it,' says Sam.

'I never knew Glenn Hoddle had a beard,' says Ella. She is now peering at an old team photo of Spurs, which Sam has desecrated.

'Why can't you sit down, Ella?' says Sam.

'Is this your Brylcreem? Didn't know you had any. Unopened as well. Typical.'

'It's all Raffy's fault,' says Sam.

'Look,' says Ella, turning towards Sam, giving up pretending to be interested in his possessions. 'If you hadn't said you were staying in tonight, he would never have come round.'

'Yeah, but I didn't know he knew they were going out. He didn't tell me.'

'Well, he wouldn't, would he?' says Ella. 'You are just so stupid.'

'Sorry,' says Sam. 'I've ruined everything, as usual.'

'Oh God, now it's pathos time.'

Sam closes his eyes. Ella goes back to wandering round the room.

'Actually, it's better in a way,' says Sam.

'How?'

'Well, having friends in,' says Sam. 'You never know, some nosey neighbours will have seen them. It'll seem more respectable, know what I mean, rather than just you and me alone in this house.'

'What does that mean?' says Ella.

'Well, I never told my mum you were coming round anyway, not that I have to, but you know . . .'

'Oh thanks a lot,' says Ella. 'You mean cos you're ashamed of me or something?'

'Oh Gawd, you know I didn't mean that,' says Sam.

'What did you mean?'

'Nothing,' says Sam.

There is another long pause. Scuffling and giggling can be heard from Sarah's bedroom next door.

'And what about your dad?' says Sam. 'You know what he's like. If he'd found out . . . The fact that you're not here alone with me, well, it'll sort of keep him happy.'

'Ecstatic probably,' says Ella.

'Look,' says Sam, 'don't get in a mood.'

'Proper Mary Poppins, aren't we,' says Ella. 'Always looking on the bright side.'

'Well, at least they all went into Sarah's room soon enough. That was something. They have left us alone.'

'Big deal,' says Ella.

'I thought that was what we wanted,' says Sam.

'What *you* wanted. Oh come on. Sit down here, just for a bit.'

'What sort of bit?' says Ella, giving half a smile.

'Tell you what,' says Sam. 'I'll give you the Brylcreem. You care more about your hair than I do. Have it, as a present.'

Ella takes off her shoes and sits on the bed beside him.

Sam's parents' bedroom

Raffy and Kirsty are in the master bedroom, forbidden territory, unbeknown to Sam. He thinks the others are all in Sarah's room, which is where he told them to go. Even worse, they are using the bed. Kirsty is under the duvet, giggling, while Raffy lies beside her, whispering in her ear.

'You know what I feel like now?' says Raffy.

'Amaze me,' says Kirsty.

'I've done that already, ain't I?' says Raffy.

'Ha ha.'

'I'm really desperate,' says Raffy.

'Not the lavatory.'

'No, it's just that, how can I put this . . .'

'Don't try,' says Kirsty.

'I'm dying for another beer,' says Raffy. 'I think there's one left upstairs.' He starts to get out of the bed, but Kirsty pulls him back in.

'Stop it. They'll hear you upstairs,' she says.

'I'll be quiet,' says Raffy. 'Don't worry.'

'But he thinks we're in Sarah's room. You're bound to make a noise. You always do.'

'I won't,' says Raffy.

'Sam will go mad if he finds out we're down here.'

'He's on the job,' says Raffy. 'He's got better things to think about.'

'Oh yeah,' says Kirsty.

'And we've helped him,' says Raffy. 'Relaxed the atmosphere, shown him the way to glory.'

'Oh well, I'd better get up as well,' says Kirsty. 'We'll have to make this bed properly so no one will ever know. And don't leave any of your things, Raffy.'

'Hold on, woman,' says Raffy, pushing her back into bed. 'One beer and I'll be straight back. Just need to refresh the parts . . .'

'You pig,' says Kirsty. 'So that's all I am, a break between beers.'

'Shush,' says Raffy. 'Now you're making all the noise.'

'*I'm* not,' says Kirsty. 'You are. Anyway, I'm getting up. Out of the way.'

'What's that?' says Raffy, looking up at the ceiling, pretending he can hear some noises above. Kirsty looks up too. Raffy then pounces, forcing her back on to the bed again. They lie there, holding on to each other, laughing and giggling.

Suddenly there is a real noise, the sound of the front door banging. Followed by the loud voice of Sam's father, in a bad temper, shouting in the hall.

Followed by the voice of his wife saying she did not want to go out anyway. Then Sam's father again, saying the food was rotten and the wine disgusting. They can be heard continuing the row as they go into the kitchen.

Immediately, there is pandemonium upstairs. Sam and Ella get out of Sam's bed, just as Dim and Colette tear into the room, still half-dressed, followed by Raffy and Kirsty, carrying their clothes. Sam turns the volume up on his stero. Raffy throws himself on the floor. The others think for a moment he may have collapsed, till he starts laughing hysterically.

Taz: a brief glimpse

EPISODE 6

The sixth-form common room,
end of another school day

Most people are getting their things in order, going through the evening rituals, slowly packing away another day, disposing of another set of classroom memories. Another Wednesday is about to be banished, leaving hardly a trace. Where do they all go?

Some people are just standing, blank, switched off, caught in a time warp in front of their lockers, trying to remember what they should be doing, what they might need for tonight, wondering what it's all about. Who are they, and where are they going, if anywhere. Last weekend is forgotten, yet a whole chasm yawns ahead before another weekend looms into sight. It's one of those dreary, anonymous mid-week days. The nights are getting dark, and it's raining. No excuse, alas, not to go straight home and get some work done.

Several students are waiting around because they hope to see Mr Witting. One or two, such as Colette, are reading old notices. Anything to put in a little bit of time rather than go directly home, to face the reality of home and homework. There is a minor flurry when Taz appears, popping her head through the common-room door, looking round as if she has forgotten something or is looking for someone.

'Hi, Taz,' shout a few chancers. 'Me, Taz,' yell others. 'I'm over here, darling,' says Raffy.

Taz looks blankly through all the boys, but she does give Colette a big smile. Then she disappears.

The Wednesday woes return, the mid-week blues. Slowly everyone finally packs up, making an effort to get their own little show of life and activity on the road again.

'I feel as if I've been in the sixth form a hundred years already,' sighs Jules. 'I can't remember what life was like before this.'

'I keep on thinking I'm missing things,' says Colette, still stuck in front of the notice board.

'Talking about me?' says Dim.

'I've given up with you,' says Colette. 'You're a washout.'

'Well, it wasn't my fault,' says Dim, getting his football boots out of the locker.

'I look at these notices,' says Colette, 'and I see all the meetings I've missed, all the activities I never took part in. Look, there was a Sixth-Form Disco. I never even knew. And a Sixth-Form Racial Policy Meeting. Missed that as well.

'Hey, Dim, did you know there's already a Christmas Party Committee? Thank Gawd I'm not on it. Don't mind going, but they'd better not give me a job. And it says here something about a Choir Rehearsal on tonight. I never even knew we had a choir. There's a whole life going on in the rest of the sixth form which I never knew about.'

'You're working too hard, Colette,' says Jules. 'That's why.'

'Oh yeah,' says Colette.

'Well, I am,' says Jules. 'Turned over a new fig leaf. The world is about to see a new me. Head down, no more frivolities.'

'Does that mean you won't come with me?' says Colette.

'Well, I shouldn't really,' says Jules.

'No use asking *him*,' says Colette, making a face towards Dim.

'I've told you,' says Dim. 'We've got a football practice.'

'Oh yeah,' says Colette. 'And that's always much more important than me.'

'Tell you what. I'll give you a bell when I get home, all right?' says Dim.

'You'd be useless anyway,' says Colette. 'You've got no taste at all, and no opinions. Wouldn't want you anyway, so stick.'

Dim snaps closed the padlock on his locker and packs his football gear into a plastic bag. He starts to leave the common room, then comes back, swinging his bag, and gives Colette a light kiss on the cheek. 'Might see you later then,' he says.

'Oh rapture,' says Colette.

'Oh rupture,' says Jules, 'if you're not careful with that bag.'

'Come on then, Jules,' says Colette. 'You will come with me, won't you? I know I can rely on you. You're the only bloke in the whole sixth form with any taste at all.'

'Okay then,' says Jules. 'But I am working terribly hard for the rest of the term. It's part of the new, deeply concerned, deeply committed Jules.'

Colette takes his arm and together they leave school.

Camden Town, half an hour later

Colette and Jules have stopped outside the Kentucky Fried Chicken restaurant.

'When you said taste,' says Jules, 'I do hope this is not what you meant.'

'You're such a snob,' says Colette.

'No, I just do have good taste.'

'Well, close your eyes,' says Colette, 'and hold my hand.'

'If I wake up in South America, tell Mr Witting my essay might be late this week,' says Jules.

Colette leads him along the pavement to the next shop, the clothes shop, then she takes her other hand away from his eyes.

'So,' says Jules. 'So?'

'Can't you see it?' says Colette. 'In the corner. Isn't that the most brilliant jacket you've ever seen?'

'Hmm,' says Jules.

'Oh, you pig,' says Colette, hitting him.

'Nice, but rather ordinary really, Colette. Not what I'd call Groovy Great, or Can't Wait To Wear You.'

'Well, I'm getting it,' says Colette. 'Don't care what you say.'

'Hmm, £79.99,' says Jules. 'I suppose that is pretty reasonable, but then it is a fairly ordinary shop. Must be ordinary, I've never even noticed it before.'

'Oh shut up,' says Colette, pressing her nose against the window.

'The leather looks good quality,' says Jules. 'If it's real.'

'Course it is, you pig.'

'I quite like the lapels,' says Jules. 'I like them big and floppy. It might be too big for you, though.'

'That's what I want,' says Colette. 'I want it big, to keep me warm in the winter. I've never had a decent winter jacket, ever.'

'Come on then,' says Jules. 'Let's get it.'

'But do you like it?'

'Course,' says Jules. 'I was just winding you up. Looks excellent. If you don't buy it, I will.'

They go into the shop together. Colette slaps down the money, exactly the right amount: seven crisp ten-pound notes, a fiver, four pound coins, plus 99p in change. She immediately puts on the jacket, already feeling she wants to keep it on for ever.

'Hey, it looks brilliant,' says Jules, as they come

out of the shop.

'Do you think so?' asks Colette.

'Yeah,' says Jules, making her stop so he can stand back on the pavement and admire it.

'Now I know who you look like.'

'Who?'

'Biggles.'

'You beast,' says Colette, pretending to hit him over the head.

'That was meant as a compliment,' says Jules. 'I really will buy it from you if you go off it. It will look brilliant with my radio cap. I can tune in and listen to all the Jerry pilots talking . . .' He pretends to be in a Spitfire, zooming back and forward across the pavement, shooting enemy aeroplanes.

'Thanks, Jules,' says Colette, giving him a kiss.

Colette's home, early evening

'Hi Mum, I'm home,' shouts Colette, opening the door of their flat. It's after five-thirty. Colette has taken her time coming home, walking the long way round, hoping as many people as possible will see her in her new, stunning leather jacket.

'Hmm, thought she'd be home by now. Rotten lot. I thought for once I could pretend I had a normal sort of mum.'

For almost all her secondary-school life, Colette has come in to an empty flat, but recently her mother has been getting home from her office quite early, sometimes by six o'clock. Colette suspects this is not because of a desperate desire to see her ever-loving daughter, but because of her mother's new boyfriend. He lives locally, so she says. Her mother is therefore keen to see him rather than hang around late at the office, doing extra work or having a drink with her office chums.

Colette goes straight to the fridge, opens it wide, the way she's not supposed to, and stares at the shelves.

'God, nothing here.' She searches all the shelves for any secret chocolate, hidden by herself, from herself. For a whole week now, she has given it up. Well, a whole two days so far. She thinks of Ella, who has come home every day of her school life to her warm and wonderful mother, bustling around, all welcoming. Ella's mother always has a little treat laid out ready on a plate, something gungy and sticky, like a rum baba, a jam doughnut, a cream bun, or a chocolate éclair. It's not fair. Ella can eat all those things and never get fat or spotty. That's even more unfair.

Colette gives another few groans, then takes half a wholemeal loaf out of the bread bin. She cuts off the mouldy edges, hacks two large slices which she fills with cucumber, salad cream and a slice of ham, then sprinkles on some chocolate chips meant to be used for cake decoration. She decides she has to have her chocolate intake somehow, just to cheer herself up.

She sniffs and wipes her nose, beginning to wonder if she's getting a cold from having walked home in the rain, then starts munching. 'This will have to do I suppose, till the old bat gets home and makes the supper. Where the hell is she anyway?'

Colette walks into her mother's bedroom, still

eating her doorstep sandwich. She hardly notices the bed unmade, all the clothes lying around. That's how her mother usually leaves her bedroom when she rushes out in the morning. She puts down the sandwich and admires herself in front of her mother's full-length wardrobe mirror, the only decent mirror in the flat.

'Biggles!' she says. 'Cheeky sod. I wonder who Biggles was anyway.' She turns round, pulling her jacket down at the back, turning it up at the collar. She tries wearing it loose with the buttons undone, casually, then completely buttoned up with the collar high. It feels good; strong, impregnable. Then she takes it off and hangs it over her shoulder, informally.

'Gawd, it is heavy. Never realized that. But there you go, Col. When you buy the best, you buy the best. None of this skimpy, artificial, man-made rubbish.' She examines the leather, feeling the depth, the weight, the richness, looking at the seams, peering into the lining. Then she lets out a scream. 'Oh my Gawd! What am I gonna do?'

She rushes to put all the lights on. She grabs her jacket, holding it up to the light, then presses it against the mirror. She has discovered two marks on the right shoulder of the jacket. Not huge, but definitely there. Two nasty blobs, like ink marks.

'Oh no,' she moans, 'I'll have to take it right back.'

She smells the marks, licks them, then studies what's left of her sandwich, just in case she might have dropped part of it on her jacket.

'Tasteless, smell-less,' she says. 'What the hell can the marks be? Well, I didn't do it. Must have been there when I bought it. That stupid Jules, he should have noticed. That's why I took him.'

Colette takes off her jacket, throws it on the bed and glares at it furiously, giving out some more moans and groans. Then she slowly picks it up again. She takes a coat-hanger from her mother's wardrobe and hangs up the jacket behind the door. She stands there angrily, as if she's going to attack it, scream at it, or at least put it in detention.

'All that bloody money,' moans Colette. 'All that money I haven't got.' She takes the jacket down and puts it on again, deciding to go out. 'Oh Gawd, look at the time. It'll be closed by now. I'm too late! Then when I take it back tomorrow after school, they won't believe me. Oh God.' Colette throws herself on her mother's bed, moaning and groaning, almost in tears, furious at her own stupidity.

The bedroom door opens. Colette screams in terror, not having seen or heard anyone coming in. It is her mother. She too looks alarmed, not knowing what all the noise is about, convinced that something really awful is happening to Colette.

'You had me worried there,' says her mother. 'Why must you dramatize everything, you silly fool. I thought it was serious.'

'It is serious,' says Colette. 'But then you don't care about me, you never have.'

'Here we go,' says her mother. 'Just the welcome home I need after a hard day.' She closes the bedroom door and leaves Colette, having noticed the untidy bed, the clothes strewn around, the uneaten sandwich. But without having noticed Colette's new jacket.

Colette: happy again

EPISODE 7

Colette's flat, an hour later

Colette's mother is preparing supper, heating up a Marks and Spencer quiche bought on the way home, and there are various salads in little plastic containers, also bought in Marks. This is to be followed by chocolate ice cream, again bought on the way home. Colette's mother does tend to eat from day to day, unless it is a special occasion. Then she might manage to plan one day ahead.

Colette is in her room doing her homework, with the door firmly closed and the stereo on as loudly as possible, just to annoy. Her mother goes into her own bedroom, tut tuts when she sees the mess, and starts to clear up.

'You might have tidied up,' she shouts to Colette.

'I can't hear you,' shouts Colette back.

'I said, considering you've made this awful mess in my bedroom, you might have had the courtesy to tidy it up.'

'What are you on about, woman?' says Colette, opening her door. 'I am trying to work.'

'This mess,' says her mother.

'I didn't make it,' says Colette, going into her mother's bedroom and looking at the bed and all her mother's clothes lying around. 'That's how you always leave it.'

'I do not,' says her mother. 'I particularly cleared it up this morning.'

'Oh yeah, I've seen you clearing up.'

'Then whose is this disgusting sandwich, miss?' Her mother picks up the remains of the crusts, plus bits of cucumber.

'Oh that,' says Colette. 'That's your fault. If you were a proper mother and had little treats for me when I came home, like proper mothers do, I wouldn't have to make stuff just to keep myself alive.'

'You've had someone in,' says her mother, looking accusingly at Colette. 'Haven't you?'

'What a terrible thing to say,' says Colette. 'You're really horrible, sometimes. Not everyone is like you, you know . . .'

'And that's enough of that,' says her mother.

'Well, you started it,' says Colette.

'Anyway, I can tell. You've had some boy in my bedroom.'

'What are you talking about?'

'This jacket,' says her mother, picking it up from the floor. 'It's Dim's, presumably.'

'It is not,' says Colette. 'And just take your scruffy fingers off it. That jacket cost me £79.'

'What?' says her mother, horrified.

'I was gonna show it to you straight away,' says Colette. 'I waited and waited, but then you came in and were horrible to me. In fact you've been horrible all the time.'

'Where did you get the money from?'

'None of your business,' says Colette. 'I do have friends you know.'

'You borrowed the money for this jacket?'

'Oh, stop going on about it, you stupid old woman,' says Colette. 'Anyway, it's going back. It's got marks on the shoulder. I'll get my money back, don't you worry. As if you cared anyway . . .'

Colette grabs the jacket from her mother, holding it up to show her the marks. They have disappeared. There are now no marks. She turns it over, inside and out, examines both shoulders, the back and the front, but there are now no marks at all.

'This is weird,' says Colette. 'There were these two sort of inky marks on the shoulder, just here, but they've gone.'

'Is it real leather?' asks her mother, feeling it.

'Course it is,' says Colette. 'The best.'

'It was probably rain,' says her mother. 'Did you get caught in that shower?'

Colette nods her head.

'Then that's all it was, you silly girl. Rain always leaves marks on real leather, unless it's been treated. Didn't you know that?'

'No,' says Colette, smiling, putting on the jacket and looking at herself in the mirror.

'You look terrific, darling,' says her mother. 'Can I borrow it sometime?'

'Not likely,' says Colette. 'I don't want it ruined.' She goes round the room, showing off the jacket. 'Do you really like it, Mum?' she asks.

'It is very nice,' says her mother. 'But the money, Colette, how could you?'

'Don't go on about it,' says Colette.

'I can't help it. Who on earth did you borrow from?'

'God, I'm glad it's okay,' says Colette, taking her jacket off and hanging it up. 'I was dead worried about those marks.'

She is smiling now, happy once again, though still upset that she should be accused of having a boy in her mother's bedroom. Her mother is pleased that Colette has recovered her normal good humour, though she is still worried about the bedroom. She feels convinced that she did tidy it up this morning.

'Supper in half an hour,' says her mother, giving Colette a hug. 'Okay, darling?'

Half an hour later

Supper is now on the table. Colette's mother has opened a tin of pâté, kept for emergencies, and made some thin, hot toast, for their first course.

'Ready, darling,' she shouts.

'Coming,' says Colette.

'Could you do me one favour?' says her mother.

'No,' says Colette, sitting down at the table. 'Not now, I'm exhausted. I've finished that stupid essay on Wordsworth, but it's useless. Just like his useless poetry. He writes like an old sheep, if you ask me.'

'That's been said before,' says her mother. 'Do you know that famous parody about him?'

'No, and I don't want to,' says Colette.

'Oh you must. It's very good. It was written by some student, after Wordsworth died. I've got it somewhere . . .'

'Oh no, sit down,' says Colette.

'Now where is it?' says her mother, getting up.

'Mother, I'm starving. Not now.'

'I must get it,' says her mother, 'while it's in my head. You might be able to use it in your essay or your A level exam. Hold on.'

Colette groans, but her mother goes to a bookshelf and starts looking for a paperback biography of Wordsworth. Colette will admit, if pressed, that her mother is quite clever and knows a lot, but she still hates her mother telling her things, telling her about books she must read, or worse, insisting on reading things out to her. 'Oh Gawd, why did I ever mention Wordsworth,' she moans.

Her mother has now found the book, and the right passage. She is determined to read it out, despite Colette's sighs and groans.

> 'There are two Voices; one is of the deep,
> And one is an old half-witted sheep,
> And Wordsworth, both are thine.'

Her mother stops, pleased with herself for remembering about the verse and then for finding it. She beams at Colette for approval.

'Not bad, I suppose,' says Colette.

'It's actually very clever,' says her mother. 'There is a famous poem of Wordsworth's which is about two voices. You must know it.'

'I don't know anything,' says Colette. 'Except that I'm starving.'

'So am I,' says her mother, sitting down.

'About time,' says Colette.

'Oh, nearly forgot,' says her mother. 'What I was going to ask you, darling, was to pop along to the off-licence and get a nice bottle of Beaujolais.'

'Oh God, why?' says Colette. 'Why can't you drink water?'

'I just feel like a drink with this meal,' says her mother. 'You and me together, it will be rather nice don't you think, hmm?'

'Well, I don't want any,' says Colette. 'And you won't get through a bottle on your own.'

'I can try,' says her mother, smiling.

'Unless you're expecting your toy boy to pop in,' says Colette.

'Look, please don't use that phrase,' says her mother. 'We've had that joke, and it's not funny.'

'I don't think it's funny either.'

'He has got a name, you know.'

'I don't want to know it,' says Colette.

'Dave, he's called. Dave King,' says her mother. 'He has this joke that he's really called Nosmo King.'

'Spare me,' says Colette.

'Do you get it? Because he doesn't smoke cigarettes. No Smoking.'

'What does he smoke then?' says Colette.

'I know you'll like him when you do meet him,' says her mother. 'He's dying to meet you.'

'Then invite him now,' says Colette, 'as you've made this huge repast. Ring him up.'

'He's not on the phone.'

'Huh. Been cut off, has he?'

'No, he's just staying with friends for the moment,' says her mother.

'Oh, he's got friends, has he?' sneers Colette.

'Tell you what,' says her mother, getting up. 'If I give you enough money, you can buy yourself some chocolate as well.'

'Don't you ever listen?' says Colette. 'I'm off chocolate. For ever.'

But her mother is not listening. She goes across to the Welsh dresser to find her purse. It is so tightly packed with credit cards, identity cards, bills and Barclaycard receipts going back for months that getting into it is like an excavation, trying to find a way into a new seam.

'Oh sugar,' says her mother. 'I've only got loose change. Get me my wallet, dear.'

'I'm not your servant,' says Colette. 'Get it yourself.'

Her mother comes back to the table, shoves some toast and pâté in her mouth, and goes to the fridge.

'It's not bad, this pâté,' she says, opening the fridge and searching inside. 'Do you remember when we got it?'

Colette does not answer.

'When I took you on that day trip to Boulogne, this time last year, no, hold on, it was during your half term. I know it was a Thursday, because I got the day off. Do you remember? We got the hover-craft and had to leave really early. We had lunch in this lovely little restaurant near the castle. With pink tablecloths. It seemed so French and intimate, yet everyone around us turned out to be English. Then we went shopping before we got the boat home, and I got this pâté. It's lasted well, hasn't it, when you consider it's almost a year old, but I always think that French things – oh my God –'

Colette's mother has stopped in mid-sentence. Colette has not been listening, so it takes her a while to register the sudden silence.

'I can't believe it,' says her mother.

She slowly takes all the food out of the middle of the fridge, then continues to stare at the emptiness for several minutes. She closes the fridge mechanically, like a clockwork toy, or an emblem from a video game working in slow motion. She turns and goes to sit down on their battered couch.

'You feeling okay, Mum?' says Colette.

'How much was your new jacket?' asks her mother, after a long pause.

'You what?' says Colette.

'The jacket. The one you bought this afternoon.'

'A bargain,' says Colette. 'That's all you have to know.'

'It was £79,' says her mother, flatly, quietly. 'You've already told me.'

'So why did you ask?'

'And you only had £19 in your bank account, didn't you,' says her mother.

'Actually it's £19.50, plus interest.'

'I had £60 in this fridge this morning,' says her mother. 'Now it's gone.'

'So?' says Colette.

'So,' says her mother.

'Whatcha looking at me like that for?'

'Colette –' begins her mother.

'Oh my God,' says Colette. 'You don't think I took it?'

'What else can I think?'

'That's the most awful thing you've ever said,' says Colette, getting up.

'Well, it was either you, or whoever you had in the flat this afternoon . . .'

'Bloody hell!' shouts Colette. 'I've already told you. I haven't been here. Nor have I taken your lousy money.'

Her mother stares at her, not accusingly any more, but sadly, almost in tears.

'God, you don't believe me!' screams Colette. 'That's the worst thing of all.'

'Colette,' says her mother. 'Just tell me the truth.'

'I've told you the truth.'

Her mother sits slumped, head down, then she looks up, as if pleading for Colette to confess so that they can forget it, and start afresh together, once again.

'If you don't tell the truth,' says her mother, 'I'll have to get the police.'

'Get the police,' says Colette. 'See if I care. I'm

getting out. I'm leaving. And you'll never see me again . . .' She rushes to the door of the flat, tears it open and runs out, banging it behind her.

Colette's mother sits for an hour, without moving. The quiche gets cold and starts to congeal. The ice cream, which had been put out to soften up, is now running over the side of the plate across the kitchen table and down on to the black and white floor tiles.

The phone rings. Colette's mother jumps up, startled.

'Hi, it's me,' says a voice. 'Ella.' She sounds bright and cheerful. 'Just to say Colette's here,' she goes on. 'But as it's so late, she's staying with me tonight. Okay? I hope the conference goes well tomorrow. Bye-ee.'

Ella: thinking ahead

EPISODE 8

Friday morning, Hampstead Heath

Jules is jogging. This time it does look for real. He is wearing old jeans, torn at the knees, tatty trainers which have split and a stained T-shirt. On his back he has a little rucksack with books in, and the radio cap is on his head. He passes the Russian ladies, who do not give him a second look, but the dog called Crumble runs after him, wanting to play. Crumble's owner is standing by the pond, staring across it through his binoculars. The dog won't leave Jules alone till he throws a stick into a pond for him.

Jules has to rest after that. He suspects he has twisted his arm, throwing the stick. He might look tougher and less arty on the outside, but inside, not

81

a lot has changed. Then he jogs off again towards school.

'Hi, man,' says Matt, coming out of the over-grown house. 'It is Jules, innit?'

'The very same,' says Jules.

'There's something different about you,' says Matt, blinking, not sure what it is.

'My cap,' says Jules. 'I usually have it tuned in the mornings to RJR, or Fresh FM or sometimes Sky, but now I'm into really heavy stuff, man. Radio 3.'

'Wicked,' says Matt. 'Is that a new pirate?'

'Yeah,' says Jules. 'They broadcast from this boat offshore near Penzance.'

They walk towards school together. Jules is quite pleased to have an excuse to slow down. Matt never does anything quickly, either walking, working or picking up remarks.

'How's the house going?' asks Jules. He has become rather intrigued about it over the last two weeks, picking up details from his occasional meetings with Matt, though he still knows little about what happens inside the house.

'Excellent,' says Matt. 'You should try it. Really excellent. No hassle.'

'Who owns the property anyway?' asks Jules.

'We do,' says Matt.

'Oh yeah.'

'And you do,' continues Matt.

'How come?' asks Jules.

'All property is theft,' says Matt. 'So we have repossessed the house for everyone.'

'So you need Marx to get in,' says Jules, regretting his smart remark as soon as he says it, knowing Matt takes things so seriously.

'No,' says Matt. 'It's open to all, just like our sixth form.'

'And just like the whole of life should be,' says Jules.

'Right,' says Matt, suddenly clapping him on the back. 'That's really good.'

Jules goes into school, hoping that the designer sun specs in his rucksack have not been broken by the tender hands of Matt.

Sixth-form common room, lunch time

Most people have finished eating. Being sixth formers, they are allowed to bring their hamburgers and chips from the dining area into the common room. Raffy is going round asking everyone the same question, but not getting very far. Jules is still talking to Matt about his squat, but not learning much. Colette is talking to Ella on their couch, but not giving much away.

'Where's she gone then, on this conference?' asks Ella.

'Dunno,' says Colette, pulling her new leather jacket tightly about her. So far, she has worn it all day and every day.

'Oh you must know,' says Ella.

'She's always going away. It used to be with her boss, but now I think it's with her new toy boy.'

'When's she back?' asks Ella.

'Dunno,' says Colette.

'You must know,' says Ella.

'Okay then,' says Colette. 'I'll tell you. She hasn't gone away anywhere. We're not talking. We've had a row. I might never go back.'

'What about?'

'Oh, the usual things. You know . . .' says Colette. Ella waits for her to explain.

'Could either of you two ladies,' says Raffy, coming over, using the word 'ladies' just to annoy, 'see your way to lending me a quid? I'm starving. Not eaten for days. Huh?'

They both ignore him.

'Oh come on,' says Raffy. 'Just till tomorrow, when I get paid. Please.'

'Get lost,' says Colette. 'I haven't got a penny. I'm in debt up to here.'

'Nor me,' says Ella.

'Jules, my old mate,' says Raffy. 'We all know *you* are loaded. How about a small fiver, eh, till tomorrow?'

'I am loaded,' says Jules. 'You're quite right.' He takes off his rucksack and hands it to Raffy. Everyone laughs.

'Good one, Jules,' says Raffy. 'Look, you must be saving a fortune at the moment, wearing those rubbish clothes instead of spending dosh on your usual gear, so how's about it, huh? Just one quid would do, a little quidlet?'

'You know the position, Raffy,' says Jules, quietly. 'I can get credit and sometimes use my old man's cards, run up certain bills on his account,

84

which his firm then pays for, but I don't actually have any spends, no ready dosh, get it?'

'Sorry, old bean,' says Raffy. 'Sorry I spoke.'

'Hey, man,' says Matt. He is pulling out all his pockets, though Raffy had not even asked him for a loan. 'If I have anything, you can have it,' he says.

Old cigarette packets, used matches, torn bits of paper, a broken plectrum, three small blue biros as supplied by betting shops, some chewing gum, then a large padlock and a bunch of keys drop on to the floor from the recesses of Matt's clothing, but no money.

'It was a kind thought,' says Raffy. 'As you are a kind person.' He lies down on the floor in his usual position, indicating heavy boredom. Most people return to their studies.

'Actually,' says Ella quietly to Colette, 'I've got something to talk to you about.'

'What?' asks Colette.

'My dad's beginning to moan a bit.'

'How do you mean?'

'You know, about you staying these last two nights. I love having you, and so does my mum, but you know what he's like. He says he wants his house to himself at the weekend. He's a pig, of course. I'm sure it will be okay on Monday, though. He's doing nights next week.'

'Don't worry,' says Colette. 'I'll go home tonight, I suppose. No alternative, really. I wish I was eighteen, and could get away somewhere, for good and all . . .'

'Yeah,' says Ella.

They both sit and think about the future, about the time when they'll go away to college, when they'll have a chance at last to live away from home, possibly in their own flat. If they ever do go away to college.

The common-room door opens and in comes Taz.

Everyone looks up, even Raffy, despite pretending to be asleep. Taz does not usually give the common room the benefit of her presence at lunch time, as she objects to the smell of cheap food. She prefers the library for quiet study, or leaves the school completely, disappearing somewhere smart, though no one knows where.

'Taz!' says Raffy, jumping up. 'My love, my own heart, my treasured one. Just the woman, I mean lady, I was looking for.'

Taz looks across the room, as if trying to locate someone, and it's certainly not Raffy. She smiles at Colette.

'Hey, love your jacket,' she says. 'It's ace.'

Then she turns to leave the common room.

'Hold on,' says Raffy. 'Could you just lend me a little bit of money, huh?'

'Money?' says Taz, as if it is a filthy word. 'I don't carry money. Who does, these days.'

She sweeps out. Raffy throws himself back on the floor, thumping the carpet in pretend fury, then giving little pants, in pretend passion.

'Hey, rot guts,' says Vinny, coming across the room. 'How much you want?' From his back pocket, he pulls out a wad of fivers.

'How much you got?' asks Raffy.

'Loadsamoney, you asshole,' says Vinny, handing Raffy a fiver. 'Just one condition. Don't lend it to any of your poncey, hippy friends. All right?'

After school

Colette, Jules and Dim are standing at the school gates.

'So where did you get the money from, Col?' asks Dim.

'I can't tell you,' says Colette.

'Oh come on,' says Dim.

'No, it's a secret,' says Colette.

'I presumed it was your own money,' says Jules.

'She hasn't got any,' says Dim. 'She's useless with money.'

'You're the useless one,' says Colette. 'You still haven't answered my question.'

'Which one?' says Dim, looking dim, though he knows full well which question it is. They have been standing at the gates for twenty minutes, with Colette refusing to let him go till he has replied to her request.

'Will you then?' she asks again.

'I dunno,' says Dim.

'But why not?' says Colette. 'You're always moaning that we have nowhere to go.'

'That's true,' says Dim.

'Well, this will be brilliant,' says Colette. 'Even Ella thinks it sounds good. No parents to worry about. Or other people's parents.'

Dim smiles at the memory, but still does not commit himself.

'What about you, Jules?' says Colette. 'It was your idea.'

'Me? Move into that place?' says Jules. 'Where would I hang my suits?'

'I thought you'd changed your image,' says Colette.

'Yeah,' says Jules. 'But not that much. That would be a *volte-face*.'

'What's that?' says Dim. 'Must be something to do with electricity.'

'Not bad,' says Jules. 'It's actually an Italian sports car. My old man has one, on the firm of course. He used to have a *sotto voce* before that.'

'Look, stop messing around, you two,' says Colette. 'This is crucial. Will you or won't you?'

'It's my mum,' begins Dim.

'Bloody hell,' says Colette. 'At your age! Can't you leave her, just for one night even? You're not normal. Families are there to be left.'

'Well,' says Dim, 'I'll think about it.'

'Do you want me to do a note for you?' says Colette. '"Please can Dmitri come to my party only it's my birthday and I want him to come and we're having ice cream and jelly and a punch in the belly and my mum will drive him home afterwards as we know he's only little and he might cry . . ."'

'Very funny,' says Dim.

'Colette's right, you know,' says Jules. 'Living in a squat is a form of party. One big party.'

'Oh yeah?' says Dim. 'Sounds dodgy to me.'

'Remember when we were all at primary school?' says Jules. 'All those good parties, those treats, the fun we had.'

'Yeah,' says Dim. 'Some of them were pretty good.'

'They were all good,' says Jules. 'But Sam's parties were perhaps the best, especially the ones in his garden, in the tree house. His mother always did fantastic things, organizing all those brilliant original games.'

'Yeah,' says Dim, thinking back.

'I used to go mad,' says Jules. 'Doing all the things I wasn't allowed to do at home, rushing up and down stairs, sliding down the banisters, tearing all over the house, hide and seek in the garden, in and out of every bedroom, building camps out of the furniture. I used to get so over-excited.'

'Sam's parties were terrific,' says Colette.

'I can still see it so clearly,' says Jules. 'Recollecting it now in tranquillity.'

'Yeah,' says Dim. 'We never have those sort of parties any more.'

'Your mum used to do OK as well,' says Jules to Colette. 'Considering.'

'Considering she's a pig,' says Colette.

'No, come on,' says Jules. 'Considering you've got hardly any room. I remember once your mum took us all in her old estate car, all ten of us, do you remember it, Dim? We went to the Heath and played on the adventure playground, then we all went to Marine Ices afterwards and had knickerbocker glories. You were sick, Colette. I think it was your eighth birthday.'

'I remember another one Sam's mother gave,' says Colette. 'It was a breakfast party, held after school. We all arrived wearing our pyjamas and went straight to bed. His mother tucked us all in, boys and girls in the same double bed, and we had cornflakes, bacon and eggs and pancakes and stuff. It was fantastic.'

'Ah, such innocence,' says Jules.

'Wish we could have those days again,' says Colette.

'Yeah,' says Dim, 'no one gives parties like that these days.'

'Most people think they're so grown up once they're in the sixth form,' says Jules. 'They assume they have to put away childish things. That's one of the big attractions of a squat. It's a chance to be retarded, in a sort of cool, adult, freaky way. Opting out, going backwards. What they're trying to do is re-create a non-stop birthday party, make an adventure playground for freaky teens who don't want to grow up.'

'Jules, you've made it sound brilliant,' says Colette. 'Just one thing. How do you know?'

'I don't,' says Jules. 'I'm just guessing. I guess.' He puts his rucksack over his back, limbers up, then starts jogging on the spot before setting off, in the direction of his home.

'Tell you what, Dim,' says Colette. 'If you do come tonight, I'll tell you my secret.'

Dim says nothing. He unlocks his bike chain,

makes his pannier secure, then gets on his bike and cycles off in the direction of his home. Colette pulls her leather jacket around herself. She too heads for home, but unlike Dim, she is telling herself it will be the last time she ever does so.

Jules: mucking in

EPISODE 9

Later that evening, outside the squat

Colette is standing inside the overgrown garden. She is wearing her leather jacket over a pink Mickey Mouse sweatshirt. In her hand she has a small case, a furry, leopardskin holdall belonging to her mother. She has been home, straight from the school gates, rushing in and out to grab a few things quickly, just in case her mother might come home early from work and find her.

Colette stares around, beginning to be slightly worried. The front door and every window is barricaded. It looks as if the house has been abandoned, yet Matt told her just a few hours ago that it was full of people, a veritable commune, a hive of fun, endless party-type activities. She looks at her watch. Almost six o'clock. That's when she told both Jules and Dim she would be here, yet there is no sign of either of them.

'Matt!' she shouts, but not too loudly. She tries to get round to the back of the house, but the garden is too overgrown. There is a doorway on either side, but both doors are securely locked. She returns to the front door and stands on the bottom step, wondering what to do next.

A large black car draws up at the front gate, stops, and a figure peers out from the back seat. Colette dashes up the front steps to a little porch, looking for cover. She notices a faded name plate, 'Boscastle House', and realizes this must once have been a handsome villa. She ducks behind some creepers, hoping no one will be able to find her. Colette knows how vulnerable young girls are in London, especially those walking on their own, carrying nothing but a little holdall. Anybody might have seen her and followed her. She could be trapped in this wild garden, outside an empty house, and no one would know.

'Why did I bring this,' she thinks, looking at her little case. 'So cheap and vulgar. Trust my mother to have something so crummy. I look as if I'm straight off the train from somewhere in darkest Yorkshire. Pocklington perhaps . . .' Colette has no idea exactly where or what Pocklington is, but the name has always struck her as funny.

The car eventually moves off. Then it stops again, about twenty metres further on. Someone can be heard getting out. Colette dodges back behind the creepers, looking for somewhere to

hide. She finds a rope and holds on to it, flatten-
ing herself against the wall so no one can see
her.

Through the broken gate, stepping with difficulty
over the fallen bricks and stones, picking his way
round the rubbish and litter, comes Jules, dragging
not just one but two suitcases, both expensive, both
matching. He is wearing a black bomber jacket that
Colette has never seen before, and what looks like a
paisley pattern shirt, or it could be acid house or
Gothic. Colette is not as good as Jules on styles
or the names for them. She thought Jules had
gone normal, into scruffy jeans like most people,
but he looks like he's dressed for a warehouse
party.

'Sorry I'm late,' says Jules. 'Took ages to get a
mini cab. My old man offered to drive me, but I
don't want him to know I'm here, or anyone else for
that matter. Can you imagine?'

A window opens high up. Matt's face appears.

'The rope,' he shouts.

Colette is confused at first. Then she looks for
the rope, the one she had been holding on to, but it's
not there any more. She looks up to where Matt's
face had been, but it's not there either. Just as she
begins to tell Jules about this funny rope, it suddenly
reappears, falling with a clunk at their feet. Tied on
the end is a key. They look around, examining the
barricaded front door, and find a lock after a while.
Slowly they open the door.

The key then disappears, hauled upward by unseen hands.

Inside the squat, Matt's room

Colette and Jules are sitting on some large, multi-coloured cushions. Jules is half-sitting, half-squatting, wondering about the dirt and germs, damp and decay, and all the funny smells. The room has a psychedelic feel to it, thanks to the way Matt has splashed every conceivable surface with lurid paints. Nothing is matching, nothing is toned in or finished. It's as if he has been using up dozens of half-empty tins, all different colours, in order to cover the ceiling, the walls and even the floor. He has poured out his fantasies on one wall, from futuristic space creatures and nightmare jungle scenes to common-or-garden sexual orgies.

'Tea,' says Matt, throwing some herbs into three filthy, chipped mugs. Even Colette looks a bit worried at this.

'Great,' she says. 'With milk, please.'

'Milk?' says Matt, looking horrified. 'Milk is your enemy.'

'Er, just one small spoonful of sugar for me,' says Jules.

'Sugar?' says Matt. 'Sugar is your enemy.'

'You seem to have a lot of enemies, Matt,' says Colette.

'The world is my friend,' says Matt, 'but people who ill-treat nature or animals or themselves are my enemies.'

Jules looks at Colette, but they manage not to smile. One half of the room has been turned into a stage, made out of wooden boxes and planks. On it, Matt has set up his music centre, an electric guitar plugged into a battery of amplifiers and speakers. He also has a set of drums, for relaxation when he's not composing on his guitar.

'What's it like living here, then?' asks Colette. She looks at the mug Matt has handed to her, trying hard not to feel sick at the sight of the debris floating on top.

'Better than home,' says Matt, grinning.

'I should think different from home is more the word,' says Jules.

'I could do nuffink at home,' says Matt. 'No music after ten at night.'

'Diabolical,' says Colette.

Jules wanders round the room, leaving his mug of tea, leaving the suspect cushions, hoping to escape the worst of the smells.

'You've made it very, er, interesting,' says Jules.

'Yeah,' says Matt.

'It's a little bit hot though,' says Colette. 'Unless it's me, or this tea.'

'Shall I turn the fire off?' asks Jules. He is peering into a huge fireplace which has been vandalized, all the ironwork removed, tiles broken off, marble cracked and the mantelpiece pulled bodily from the wall. It is empty, except for an old-fashioned two-bar electric fire. Jules looks horrified as his eyes follow a worn, dangerous-looking electric flex, which goes from the back of the fire across the room and disappears under the door.

'No,' says Matt. 'You can't turn the fires off. We

have them on all the time. It's one of the King's rules.'

'Who is the King?' says Colette.

'He's upstairs. He's the King of the Castle. It's his joke, cos this house was called something Castle.'

'Yeah, I noticed that,' says Colette.

'It was a lovely house,' says Jules, 'at one time.'

'What you mean?' says Matt. 'It was rubbish. Full of capitalist stuff. They even had bells for servants. Wicked. We've made it so much better. We're all equal now, equal shares.'

'But what about the King, and his rules,' says Jules. 'Is he equal?'

'He's a benevolent despot,' says Matt. 'Come on, I'll take you to him. He'll tell you which room you can have . . .'

The squat, somewhere inside

Matt unlocks his own door, which has several padlocks, and leads Colette and Jules down a bare corridor and up some stairs. There are no banisters, all having been removed. As they go up through the house they notice that about half the rooms are padlocked and obviously used, like Matt's, and the rest are totally empty, with no door knobs, no doors, sometimes not even a door frame. All fittings have been removed, big or small, from handles and knobs to complete ceilings.

At the top of the house they come to a door on a landing. On the door are painted the words 'King of the Castle'. Matt knocks and waits. The door opens.

Matt beckons them in, then goes back down the stairs, leaving Colette and Jules to go inside on their own.

The King's premises, his little kingdom, consist of the whole of the top floor. He has somehow knocked five attic rooms together, using a hammer by the look of it, or just his own fist. Jagged edges, broken battens and hanging slivers of ancient mortar show where the walls have been taken apart. The total effect, though, is cool and clean, as all the walls have been emulsioned white, with no decorations, no paintings. The floorboards and the ceiling have been painted black.

'Hi, Colette,' says a voice from behind a screen. 'Welcome to the Castle.'

The King appears, wearing a black kimono. He is tall with long, dark hair, worn in a pigtail at the back. He is older than Colette expected, presuming he would be Matt's age; he must be almost thirty. She is surprised he should know her name, but pleased by the welcome.

'I like your collections,' says Jules, looking around, taking in all the open-plan areas which were formerly attic rooms. In one corner, he has noticed a neat row of doors, stacked against a wall. In another, a pile of wrought-iron fireplaces. He goes over to examine some wooden, Adam-style mantelpieces. Beside them, in boxes, he can see brass door handles, taps, knobs. Elsewhere there are wooden ornaments, stair rails, wooden poles. One area is totally devoted to parts of cornices, ornamental roses, all ripped straight out of ceilings.

'Have they all come from here?' asks Jules.

'Are you crazy?' says the King. 'They come from, let's say, all over. Once a house is empty, wherever it is, we strip it. Or sometimes when it's not empty.'

'You mean you've stolen all this,' says Jules.

'What is this?' says the King, smiling at Colette. 'Who's your friend?'

'It's so hot in here as well,' says Jules. He looks around and sees that there are five electric fires on, scattered throughout the top floor.

'Yeah, we're getting our own back,' says the King. 'We've been ripped off all our life, now it's our turn.'

'But the bills will be enormous,' says Colette. 'Do we all have to pay a share? I've actually got no money at the moment.'

'Nobody pays,' says the King. 'I've fixed it. Till they find out, then some sod will come and cut us off. Like they cut off the gas, the bastards.'

'Are you sort of official squatters?' asks Colette.

'Yeah, the Council knows we're here. But don't give this address for your dole money. It's too familiar. I'll give you one you can use.'

'So you don't have a job?' says Colette.

'You must be joking,' says the King. 'They only want you to do rubbish jobs, that's all this Government offers. Their intention is to keep you down, humiliate you.'

'True,' says Colette, but without really listening.

'They want you to take a job, any job, and stupid people do, because they've been conned into believing there's such a thing as the dignity of labour. That worked in the old days, when people got brainwashed into being obedient by the so-called work ethic. Now we know the truth. Work is exploitation.'

'Oh I don't know,' says Jules. 'Some occupations must be fun. Pop stars, footballers, fashion designers, selling leather jackets . . .'

'Totally manipulated,' says the King. 'They've been brainwashed. They are controlled by accountants. Those are the people behind the scenes who make the real money.'

'That's what Dim wants to do,' says Colette. 'Get behind the scenes, making all the money.'

'Who's Dim?' asks the King.

'My sort of, er, boyfriend,' says Colette. 'Is it okay if he comes as well?'

'No problem,' says the King. 'We don't have rent books here, not like Camden Council, exploiting the poor. They shouldn't own anything. They just let this house run down. We're the ones who've saved it. They don't deserve it. They've never done anything for us.'

'But they are us,' says Jules. 'They represent us.'

'Bullshit,' says the King. 'They represent themselves. They don't care about us. They're just like the Government, or Big Business, the multinational companies, the City. We're just numbers. We don't count.' He walks across the floor and opens a cupboard door. Inside, a sequence of bells is arranged on a large mahogany board, marked Kitchen, Cellars, Dining Room, Bedrooms. He pulls a bell marked Bedroom 3.

'Not bad, is it?' says the King. 'Hasn't been used

for years. I was gonna flog it, but thought I could use it here, after British bloody Telecom found out about our phone line and cut us off. At least we have internal communications, if not external. And that's what matters most, don't you agree, Jules? It's the inner man that matters.'

The door opens and in comes Matt.

'Matt,' says the King. 'We want some wine for the inner man, and inner woman. A welcome drink for my new friends. Get round to the off-licence. Some Beaujolais, I think. None of their rubbish.'

The King goes behind another screen which conceals a little kitchen area. He goes to a fridge and takes out a plastic-covered wallet. On the front are the words 'Caribbean Connections'.

'We're in funds,' he says, taking out some ten-pound notes. 'Get as much as you can, Matt. I think we'll have a party tonight, to celebrate your arrival in the Castle. You will join us, won't you, folks?'

Dim: here at last

EPISODE 10

The squat, much later that night

The party is over, at least for Jules and Colette. They have had enough and are now in their room on the ground floor at the back of the house, lying in separate heaps, slumped and exhausted. It is almost dark, except for the light from their electric fire. They have managed to rig up a door, supplied by the King, and collect a few dusty rugs, cushions and curtains which they have spread around the bare floor to make it slightly more comfortable. They don't yet have a padlock, and Jules has still not opened his cases.

Outside their room they can hear loud music throughout the rest of the house, shouts and screams, crashes and banging, as the party continues with little sign of stopping.

'I'm knackered,' says Colette. 'Gawd knows what I had to drink.'

'That music is driving me mad,' says Jules. 'I now feel a certain sympathy with Matt's parents.'

'But it is good,' says Colette, 'having no parents at all. You must admit it.'

'Oh yeah, great fun,' says Jules.

'And it is warm.'

'That also worries me,' says Jules. 'It's so dangerous, all these electric fires. I'm sure something awful will happen.'

'You're such a worrier, Jules,' says Colette. 'I never realized that till now.'

'Not a worrier,' says Jules. 'Just practical. Which is more than you are. You haven't even brought any clothes with you.'

'Let's not argue,' says Colette. 'I've had enough of arguing. That's why I came here.'

'Can't remember why I came,' says Jules. 'Remind me.'

'Shush,' says Colette, 'I'm trying to go to sleep.'

'I never will,' says Jules, turning over on his makeshift bed. 'Not with that racket.'

'Will you settle down and shut up,' says Colette.

'Oh God, now I want to go to the lavatory,' says Jules.

'You'll be lucky.'

Jules gets up and switches on the light, which makes Colette moan. She can hear him staggering down the corridor, then there is a loud shout, some more bangings and crashing, and he staggers back into the room.

'Broken,' he says. 'Some joker has smashed up

the whole lavatory. I'll have to use the window. I know it's disgusting, sorry.'

He unfastens the shutters and opens the window. Just at that moment, the electric fire goes off. It seems pitch black at first, but there is a thin shaft of London night light coming through the window, just enough for them to see.

'Close your eyes,' says Jules. 'And your ears. God, I hate the squalor of all this . . .'

'Stop moaning,' says Colette.

Suddenly there is a loud shriek from Jules, the loudest shriek of the whole night so far. Colette immediately opens her eyes to see him running round and round the room, shouting and screaming.

'A rat! A bloody rat. I've stepped on it! Oh my God . . .'

Colette looks round the room, but can see no rat. When she turns back, she can see no Jules either. He has jumped out of the window and disappeared. Colette is confused. She drank too much at the King's party and has been half asleep throughout her conversation with Jules. She realizes that the electric fire has gone off and begins to feel very cold.

'My jacket,' she thinks. 'Thank God for my jacket.' Leaning out of the makeshift bed, she manages to drag over her leather jacket. She pulls it over herself, covering her ears to keep out the noise. She soon feels warm under its weight, and falls asleep.

The squat, same room, later

The shouts and screams have stopped. The electric
guitar and stereo music ceased once the electricity
failed, but the sound of someone on the drums can
still be heard, playing the same rhythm, over and
over again.

Colette wakes up, looks around and shakes her
head, trying to work out where she is. Has she
imagined everything, is she having a dream, or is it a
nightmare? In the semi-darkness, she makes out
two cases in a corner, beside a pile of old blankets.
She can see an aerial, which she slowly follows with
her eye till it turns into a baseball cap. Then she
remembers Jules. He must have left in a hurry.

She lets her head drop, sinking into a sort of
drowse, but the noise of the drums is stopping her
from going back to sleep. She tries to analyse the
drumming, wondering if it is all in her head, which
feels about to burst. Then she remembers Matt.
She groans, and falls back on to her cushions.

The next time Colette awakens, she is dreaming
of the smell of fresh coffee, a cup being placed by
her bedside and her mother telling her to wake up,
it's time for school, she'll be late. She half-opens
her eyes, seeing a figure in front of her. She starts to
form a smile, to say 'Hi, Mum,' then lets out a
scream. The figure is not her mother. It is a man,
climbing through the open window . . .

Meanwhile, in the garden of the squat

Jules has got out of the house quickly enough, and
escaped the rat, if it was a rat. But he is now lost. He

has landed on a terrace leading into a jungle of a back garden which appears to have no exit.

'Oh God, why did I come,' says Jules to himself. 'I should never have agreed. I just felt sorry for Colette. I must have been mad. And, oh no, I've forgotten my cases.'

He finds a doorway at the side of the house and starts to climb up and over the door. On the top of it, he listens, then gingerly lowers himself over.

'Ohhhh no,' he yells.

Something has happened to his leg, though he's not sure what. His yells die away as he realizes he is not in fact in pain. His leg is still intact. No blood, no breakages. So what can it be? At first he feared he was treading on the rat, about to bite him, but now all he can feel is a warm, wet, soggy sensation. He looks below him into the front garden and can hear the sound of heavy panting. Carefully he puts his hand down to check his leg, and feels wet fur, then a wet mouth, nuzzling his hand.

'Crumble!' exclaims Jules. The golden retriever at once gets all excited, wanting a stick thrown.

Jules looks around, his eyes getting used to the first streaks of dawn, his senses soaking up the leafy, moisty smells and shivers of the early-morning autumn mists, floating across from the Highgate ponds. Over at the front of the garden, near the gate, Jules can make out the figure of Crumble's owner, dressed as always in a neat suit, his binoculars trained on the house.

'MI5,' thinks Jules. 'I should have guessed it.'

He drops down into the back garden again. He listens and waits, but Crumble has gone.

Jules makes his way through the jungle round to the other side of the house, where there is an identical doorway, also securely locked. He climbs up on to it and carefully looks over the top. He is about to lower himself to the ground when he notices two figures beneath him, large and squat, who are bending down with their backs towards him. He stops himself just in time.

Jules listens carefully, and realizes they are Russians, two of the women he regularly sees on the Heath. They have their green Marks and Spencer plastic bags beside them. They gabble in Russian for a bit, speaking into walkie talkies, then they put the machines into their carrier bags.

'What the hell is going on?' thinks Jules. 'The MI5 bloke must think the squat is Russian-controlled, while the Russians think it's an MI5 cover, to spy on them. It's all mad.'

He drops back into the rear jungle and lies in the bushes, thinking, trying to remember a story he once read in the *Hampstead and Highgate Express*.

'I suppose it's no madder than MI5 using a double-glazing bloke to spy on the Russians. Well let them play their dopey games. I certainly don't want to get mixed up in them.'

Jules makes his way to the back of the back garden this time, hoping there is a way out, but fearing it will lead into another private garden, possibly even the Russian residence.

'What if they've seen me with my radio cap on?

Oh no, they'll think I'm up to something. Probably suspect I'm IRA. And where have I left it anyway? Oh God, wish I'd stayed in my own little bed.'

He reaches a rear wall, broken-down and crumbling, too high for him to climb. He works his way along the length of it and finds a large tree. Jules begins to climb the tree, but as he does so, heavy objects start falling on his head.

'Oh no! I'm being attacked!'

Huge apples are bouncing all around him. Some of them do hit his head, but most land like hand grenades on the wall, where they splatter and split. Others disappear with a dull, heavy thud into the undergrowth on the other side of the wall. A voice cries out in agony from the same undergrowth. There follow the sounds of swearing and rustling. Jules stops climbing and sits still on a branch, not daring to breathe. There is silence for a while, then the biggest apple of all, the last one on the largest branch, decides to make a break for gravity and throw itself in a wild free-fall, determined to hit land with the maximum of schplatter and the greatest of schplits. Only it does not hit the earth, not directly. It scores a bull's eye on a human bonce.

'Oh God, I've been mugged,' shouts a voice from below. There is a lot of moaning and groaning, followed by whispering.

'That's it, Vinny,' sobs the voice. 'I'm going home.'

'Don't be stupid,' says Vinny. 'It's only an apple. Are you chicken or something? Once we're over this wall, we'll get them. Those fairies and hippies in that squat won't know what's hit them. They've got it coming to them. Come on, it's gonna be dead easy. They'll all be asleep . . .'

Jules sits very still in the tree, wondering what he should do. If he goes back, he might walk into the Russians or MI5. He would prefer not to get involved in an international incident. On the other hand, if he goes forward, he could find himself in the middle of a little local domestic difficulty.

The squat, back inside

Colette's heart feels as if it has stopped. For a moment, her spine seems to have turned to ice. Then she recognizes the figure climbing athletically through the open window.

'Sorry, Col,' says Dim. 'Had to work late.'

'Oh my God,' says Colette. 'I nearly died.'

Dim drops down beside her, taking her in his arms, holding her for reassurance, cuddling her till she stops shaking. He listens. He too can hear the drumming. Then he looks down at Colette. She is fast asleep.

'Col,' says Dim. 'Wake up. I've something to ask you. This is important.'

'Ugh,' says Colette.

'Your mother has called in the police. She's been on the phone to Ella about it. Did you take the money or not?'

'Course not,' says Colette.

'Then where did you get it from?'

'Promise you won't tell?' says Colette. 'I said I would keep it a secret.'

'Promise,' says Dim.

'From Taz,' says Colette. 'Just a loan. I'm paying her back next month, from my allowance. She doesn't want people to know she's got money.'

'How stupid,' says Dim. 'Everyone knows she's got money. That's one of the many reasons everyone fancies her.'

'You pig,' says Colette. Then she falls asleep.

Dim sits up for a while, thinking, then he too falls asleep, just as the drumming ceases.

Neither Dim nor Colette notice a rather unathletic figure, climbing slowly through the window. It is Jules. He can find nowhere else to lay his sleepy head.

'Might as well stay here till later,' he says to himself, crawling on to the pile of cushions, cuddling a body for warmth. 'I'll take my cases with me this time.'

Jules smiles, falling asleep. 'And my radio cap.'

The squat, later that morning

A strong, bright, autumn sun is streaming into the room. Colette is humming in her sleep, holding tightly on to her leather jacket. Jules is smiling in his sleep, holding on to Dim. Dim is grunting, having scored three goals at Wembley, one after extra time.

Colette wakes up from her nice dream and sniffs. 'Hmm, lovely coffee,' she says. 'Hi, Mum.'

Then she frowns as her eyes focus properly and she remembers where she is. She looks beside her and sees both Dim and Jules. She starts to get up, shivering as she feels the cold, bare floor.

'Hey, no need to hurry, darling. There's no school today.' It *is* her mother, coming through the doorway. She is carrying a large Thermos jug full of real coffee.

Colette rushes across the room, into her mother's arms.

'I'm so sorry, Colette,' says her mother. 'How can you ever forgive me?'

'No, it was all my fault,' sobs Colette.

'No, it was *my* fault, darling,' says her mother. 'I should have remembered I'd given Dave a key to the flat. The police picked him up last night with my wallet on him. And Ella told me where you were in the end. In *his* house. He hasn't touched you, has he? The lying, deceitful bastard . . .'

'Hey, what's going on here?' says Dim, waking up. He pushes Jules away.

They all have coffee and slowly get dressed and pack up all their belongings. Colette's mother has parked her old estate at the front door. Jules and Dim get in the back, while Colette sits at the front with her mother.

'Good news from Mrs Batty,' says Colette's mother as she swings the car into St Andrews Road.

'What?' says Colette, trying to remember who Mrs Batty is.

'Your essay on Wordsworth,' says her mother. 'She's given you an A. She thinks it's the best you've ever done. And she hopes you'll keep it up . . .'

In the next S.T.A.R.S. story, discover how Kirsty makes out in the photographer's studio, and whether Jules is about to become big in the media. Dim, our chunky hero, is on the verge of making serious money, but will Raffy ruin everything with his post-match celebrations? Or can Dim manage to rescue them all?